TEXAS REBELS:
ELIAS

———

LINDA WARREN

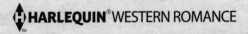

HARLEQUIN® WESTERN ROMANCE

Recycling programs
for this product may
not exist in your area.

ISBN-13: 978-0-373-75786-2

Texas Rebels: Elias

Printed in U.S.A.

Two-time RITA® Award–nominated author **Linda Warren** has written over forty books for Harlequin. A native Texan, she's a member of Romance Writers of America and the RWA West Houston chapter. Drawing upon her years of growing up on a ranch, she writes about some of her favorite things: Western-style romance, cowboys and country life. She married her high school sweetheart and they live on a lake in central Texas. He fishes and she writes. Works perfect.

Books by Linda Warren

Harlequin Western Romance

Texas Rebels

Texas Rebels: Egan
Texas Rebels: Falcon
Texas Rebels: Quincy
Texas Rebels: Jude
Texas Rebels: Phoenix
Texas Rebels: Paxton

Harlequin American Romance

The Cowboy's Return
Once a Cowboy
Texas Heir
The Sheriff of Horseshoe, Texas
Her Christmas Hero
Tomas: Cowboy Homecoming
One Night in Texas
A Texas Holiday Miracle

Visit the Author Profile page at Harlequin.com for more titles.

To my editor, Kathleen Scheibling,
for her patience, understanding and
support during a rough year.
Thank you!

Prologue

My name is Kate Rebel. I married John Rebel when I was eighteen years old and then bore him seven sons. We worked the family ranch, which John later inherited. We put everything we had into buying more land so our sons would have a legacy. We didn't have much, but we had love.

The McCray Ranch borders Rebel Ranch on the east and the McCrays have forever been a thorn in my family's side. They've cut our fences, dammed up creeks to limit our water supply, and shot one of our prize bulls. Ezra McCray threatened to shoot our sons if he caught them jumping his fences again. We tried to keep our boys away, but they are boys—young and wild.

One day Jude and Phoenix, two of our youngest, were out riding together. When John heard shots, he immediately went to find his boys. They lay on the ground, blood oozing from their heads. Ezra McCray was astride a horse twenty yards away with a rifle in his hand. John drew his gun and fired, killing Ezra instantly. Both boys survived with only minor wounds. Since my husband was protecting his children, he didn't spend even one night in jail. This escalated the feud that still goes on today.

The man I knew as my husband died that day. He couldn't live with what he'd done, and started to drink

heavily. I had to take over the ranch and the raising of our boys. John died ten years later. We've all been affected by the tragedy, especially my sons.

They are grown men now and deal in different ways with the pain of losing their father. One day I pray my boys will be able to put this behind them and live healthy, normal lives with women who will love them the way I loved their father.

Chapter One

Elias: the fourth son—the fighter.

The cowboy's last fight.

If hell froze over, Elias Rebel would be standing right there enjoying the cool breeze. Just about every woman in Horseshoe, Texas, over the age of eighteen and under the age of forty, had said those words to him at one time or another.

Work. Beer. Women. That defined Elias. A lot of people said he was different than his brothers. But he didn't care what people thought. He was who he was, doing things his way and on his terms.

After a full day of work, Elias was dog tired and headed for Rowdy's beer joint, his favorite place to unwind. He sat at a table with his booted feet propped on a chair, a cold Bud Light in his hand. With anticipation, he contemplated the bleached blonde in a corner booth. Tight skinny jeans clung to her rounded hips and long legs. A low-cut knit top hugged her breasts and he could see cleavage all the way to Dallas. Yep. Just his type.

There was just one small problem: the Dwayne Johnson–type guy sitting across from her. In jeans, boots, a leather vest and a T-shirt with a pack of cigarettes rolled up in a sleeve, the biker dude had tattoos running up his arms that made his

bulging muscles more pronounced. With one blow the guy could probably kill him.

There was nothing Elias liked more than a good fight, especially if the prize was the blonde. But sometimes common sense prevailed, even with Elias.

She glanced his way and smiled. He lifted his beer in response. Things were looking up.

Just then the front door opened and the six o'clock June sunlight bolted into the dark bar like a flash of lightning. It was blinding. Elias blinked and turned his head toward the door. The woman silhouetted there had strawberry blonde hair and he would have known her anywhere. She sashayed her pretty butt to the bar to talk to Bob, the owner of Rowdy's.

Forgetting the blonde, Elias got to his feet and made his way over to her. "Well, well, if it isn't the long-lost Maribel McCray."

"Go away, Elias," she replied without even looking at him, the way she used to do in high school.

"Oh, she remembers my name and even my voice."

"Go away, Elias," she said again, still not looking at him. Her full attention was on Bob.

"Are you sure you haven't seen him?" she asked Bob.

"No, Maribel. Young boys don't come in here."

Digging in the big purse slung over her shoulder, she pulled out a pen. She reached for a napkin and wrote on it, and then pushed it toward Bob. "That's my number. Please call if you see him."

"Sure thing, Maribel." Bob eased the napkin toward himself. "It's nice to have you back in Horseshoe."

She turned and walked out without another word. If there was a sexier woman, Elias hadn't met her. In school, with thick hair hanging down to her hips and a figure that was made for a young boy's dreams, she had personified

hotness. She hadn't changed, except her hair was shorter and in a ponytail.

"What did she want?" Elias asked.

"She's looking for her son."

Elias rested his forearms on the bar, twirling his can of beer. "She has a son. She must've gotten married. Wonder where she's been all these years."

"I didn't ask, Elias."

In high school, Elias had had a big crush on Maribel, but she hadn't given him the time of day, which was just as well since she was a McCray and he was a Rebel. There was something about attraction, though, that transcended family feuds.

She'd left school mysteriously in April before graduation and everyone had wondered what had happened to her. The rumor was she had gotten pregnant and her dad, Ira McCray, had kicked her out of the house. The other rumor was she'd run off to get married. The rumor mill in Horseshoe was alive and buzzing like bees around a honeypot. A lot of people had felt its sting. Even though Elias didn't listen to rumors, he knew certain women thrived on them. That's the way it was in a small town. But soon everyone had forgotten about Maribel McCray. What was she doing back in town?

Then it hit him. Elias's brother Phoenix had married Rosemary McCray and Rosemary, or Rosie as everyone called her, was having a difficult pregnancy. She was confined to bed until the birth in late August. Maribel must've come home to help her sister. Funny, his brother had never mentioned it.

"Why are you so curious?" Bob asked, wiping a spot on the bar. Bob was a former marine, built solid and stout. Over six feet with a growl in his voice, not many patrons dared to question him when they were asked to leave, un-

less they were drunk as a skunk. "Since Phoenix and Paxton married McCrays, it's been peaceful here in Horseshoe. I, for one, would like it to stay that way."

Bob was right. The McCray women had infiltrated the Rebel family and everything was going smoothly. Elias hoped, like everyone in Horseshoe, that the feud was dying. A lot of bitterness and resentment still lingered on the McCray side. His father had shot Ezra McCray years ago in self-defense, and the McCrays had held on to revenge like the devil holds on to a sinner. Time was passing, though, and maybe old wounds were healing.

Bob placed his hands on the bar. "What are you doing in here so early?"

Elias took a swig from the can. "I've been up since four getting hay off the field. I came here to relax. Besides, it's like a nursery at the ranch. Babies and pregnant women everywhere."

"You're the lone bachelor, Elias. When are you going to change that?"

Elias chuckled. "Never. I like my freedom."

"Did I tell you Tammy Jo's getting married?"

Elias looked at his beer and not at Bob. Tammy Jo was Bob's only child and she and Elias had been an item for a couple of years, seeing each other when she'd come home from Austin. Bob had never found out. Tammy Jo had wanted to get married and Elias hadn't, so their fun weekends had stopped. Part of him would miss Tammy Jo and the good times they'd had. But deep down he had known he wasn't the man for her. He wasn't sure if he was the man for any woman. Like he'd told Bob, he enjoyed his freedom and didn't want to be tied down.

"She's marrying an accountant and he has a good job in Austin. I hope they start having babies soon. My wife and I can't wait for a grandchild."

"Congratulations, Bob. You deserve a house full of grandkids."

The biker couple got up and walked toward the door. The blonde looked back and smiled at Elias.

"That could get you killed," Bob remarked.

"Ah, I can take him."

"In your dreams."

The door opened again and Wyatt Carson, the sheriff, walked in. Wyatt came straight to Elias. "Thought I might find you here."

It wasn't a good thing when the sheriff came looking for you. "What's up?"

"I have a stack of parking tickets on my desk that need to be paid as soon as possible."

"Wyatt." Elias sighed. "You're not going to bring that up again."

The sheriff tipped back his hat. "It's against the law to park in the fire zone at the courthouse. Yet you continue to do so despite my warnings and Stuart's."

"When was the last time you had a fire at the courthouse?"

"None that I can recall."

"See? I'm not endangering anyone. The auto-parts store is right across the street and there's never any parking. I park to the side and run to the store. It takes ten minutes, tops. But Stuart always manages to ticket my truck. Next time I see him I'm gonna put a knot on his head."

"Then I'd have to arrest you."

"Come on, Wyatt, what do you want from me?"

"I want you to pay the tickets, but I know you're stubborn and you're not going to do that. So I've got a better solution."

"And what would that be?"

"I need someone to do undercover work."

Elias laughed out loud and slapped the bar with his hand. "I'm not a cop and I don't want to be one. That's your job."

"Okay, Elias, I'm going to give you a choice. Jail or undercover work. Teenage boys are stealing beer around Horseshoe. They've hit the grocery store, the convenience store and this place."

Elias looked at Bob. "You didn't mention that."

Bob shrugged. "Wyatt said not to tell anyone because he wants to catch 'em."

"Have you checked out the Kuntz boys, Wyatt?" If anything was stolen in Horseshoe, Freddie, his brother Scooter and cousin Leonard were always at the top of the list. They lived in a run-down trailer on the outskirts of town. Their mother worked nights in a bar and the boys were left to fend for themselves. Elias had given them rides. Sometimes late at night.

"It's not them. The school called CPS and they're checking into their home situation. But the mother always pulls a rabbit out of her hat at the last minute. The sister has now moved in and she's supposed to be there for the boys at night. CPS has backed off, but I'm keeping a close eye on the boys. I was talking to them when I got the call about the convenience store."

Elias sighed. "I'm almost afraid to ask, but what do you want me to do?"

"Keep an eye out while you're in here."

"Come on, Wyatt, I'm not ratting out kids."

"They're stealing. And that's against the law and I've sworn to uphold the law."

"You're a stickler for right, aren't you?"

Wyatt nodded. "Yes, I am. What's your answer? Jail or undercover work?"

Elias knew he didn't have much choice, but he would

hold out to the last minute. "Exactly what do you want me to do?"

"I want you to watch the door. One of the boys is coming through the front and slipping past the bar to the back. He then opens the back door and lets the other two in and they take the beer and run. You have to stay sober and alert me if you see someone going into the back room. That's it. I'll take it from there. All you have to do is call if you see someone."

"I don't know." He hated to turn on kids. He'd once been a wild teenager and beer had always been a temptation.

"Then I'll have to arrest you. You can sit out your time and do community service. I believe the senior citizen center needs mopping and cleaning. That would be a good job for you."

"Wyatt, it's hay season on the ranch and—"

"I'll sweeten the deal. When you have to go to the auto-parts store, you can park in the sheriff's area." He held up a finger. "But just ten minutes, and I'll alert Stuart not to ticket you."

Now there was a deal. He held out his hand. "Deal."

Wyatt shook his hand. "Stay alert tonight and tomorrow. It's usually Saturday night when they hit. Thanks."

"Yeah, right." Elias grimaced.

"Look at it this way," Bob said. "You'll be sitting down here instead of in a jail cell."

Elias spent the evening watching the door and it was as much fun as watching grass grow. The night was slow and nothing was happening so at 10:30 p.m. he went home. He had a full day tomorrow and he needed some sleep. Getting into his truck, he felt a pang of…loneliness. It couldn't be. He was never lonely, but sometimes *lonely* crept into his soul without warning.

At six o'clock the next evening, Elias came through the back door dirty and tired, hay stinging him around his collar and down the back of his shirt. He needed a shower and a beer. Grabbing one out of the refrigerator, he took a moment to pop the top.

"Elias?" Grandpa called.

He lived with his grandpa and was the official caretaker of the old man who aggravated him more than anyone. Quincy was Grandpa's favorite and he'd usually done the caregiving until he got married. After that, somehow the responsibility for Grandpa fell on Elias's shoulders. He wasn't the nurturing kind, but he and Grandpa managed to get along.

He walked into the living room. Grandpa sat in his chair with his dog, Mutt, on his lap. Nearing eighty, Grandpa had snow-white hair and a booming voice known to stop his grandsons in their tracks.

"What's up?"

Grandpa handed him the remote control. "Get the Western channel. I can't find it."

Elias took a deep breath. "I wrote it down—" he pointed to the pad on the end table by Grandpa "—right there."

"Ah, if you don't want to help me then don't." Grandpa tended to be grouchy at times and he liked being pampered.

Elias took the control and flipped it to the Western channel. "Satisfied?"

"Thank you."

Elias shook his head. One little thing made his grandpa happy. He headed for the bathroom. "Are you going to Quincy's for supper?" he asked over his shoulder. Quincy still helped with Grandpa, as did his other brothers.

"Yes, I'm waiting on him. He's gonna pick me up so I don't have to drive in the dark."

Quincy lived across the pasture and it wasn't that far

from Grandpa's house. Grandpa just liked the attention and that was fine. He had to get to Rowdy's.

THIRTY MINUTES LATER, he was sitting at a table, watching the door on a Saturday night. It was like blowing up balloons, boring as hell. He looked around at the rustic beer joint where he spent a lot of his time. He never really noticed his surroundings. The joint had been in Horseshoe forever and had been run by several people. Bob had owned it for the past fifteen years. The worn hardwood floors and the jukebox were probably as old as Elias. The songs hadn't changed in years. Neon beer signs decorated the back of the bar. Red booths lined one wall and had gray duct tape to cover the holes. Above the booths were posters of country music stars who had stopped by. In the back room, there was a pool table. A lot of guys hung out in there.

The place was filling up fast. Dee and Tracy, the waitresses, were working hard to keep up with the beer orders. Someone slipped a quarter in the jukebox and George Strait's "A Fire I Can't Put Out" came on. Two couples got up and started dancing. It was Saturday night at Rowdy's.

Dee stopped by his table. "What are you doing over here by yourself?"

He held up his beer. "Drinking."

"Want another?"

"Nah, I'm good." He hadn't drunk any of the beer. He wanted to be alert like Wyatt had said. The trouble was Wyatt could never tell if Elias was drunk or not. Elias could hold his beer. Everyone knew that. But tonight, for once, he was following the rules. He should write that down on a calendar somewhere.

Couples were still coming in the door and there wasn't much room for anybody else. Suddenly he saw something

out of the corner of his eye. Two couples were standing at the door and there seemed to be someone behind them. Then the figure was gone. Elias got up and went through the swinging half-door of the bar to the back room. Peering around the corner, he saw a guy open the back door. This was it.

He pulled out his phone and called Wyatt. "They're here."

"Don't do anything, Elias. I'm on my way."

Elias tucked his phone back into his pocket, walked out the front door and made his way around to the back. He crouched in the bushes and watched as three figures carried beer through the wooded area to a vehicle. Elias crept closer. The kids were laughing as they stored the beer in the back of an SUV.

"I slipped in and out and that old coot never saw me," one bragged.

Another one said, "Now we can par-ty."

Wyatt had better hurry or the kids were going to be gone. Just then headlights flashed from the right and from the left. Sirens blared as they pulled up to the SUV. Wyatt's patrol car was in the back and Stuart's in the front. The car revved up and the kid tried to go around Stuart's car, but Stuart pulled his car over and blocked him.

Wyatt got out of his car with a megaphone. "Turn off the engine. Turn off the engine. Now!"

In response, the kid revved it up again and tried to go around Stuart's car without any luck.

"Get out of the car!" Wyatt shouted. "If you don't get out, I'm going to shoot out the tires. You have thirty seconds."

No response.

Wyatt pulled his gun from his holster. The driver's door of the SUV slowly opened and a kid crawled out with a

hoodie over his head. Two other kids crawled out from the other side.

"Line up against the car," Wyatt ordered, still holding the gun in his hand. "Frisk them," he said to Stuart.

Stuart did as he was told. "No weapons."

Wyatt shoved his gun into his holster and pulled a flashlight from his car. He shined the light in the first boy's face. "Brandon Polansky, your parents are going to be proud of you."

The thing about a small town was everyone knew everyone, and Wyatt knew the people better than most.

Wyatt stepped over to the second boy. "Billy Tom Wentz, this is going to be a shock to your parents and your grandfather."

Billy Tom hung his head.

Before Wyatt could reach the third boy, he leaped over the hood of the car and bolted for the woods. Elias reached out with one arm and snagged him, wrestling him to the ground. The kid came up fighting with both arms. He was skinny and tall, but he didn't have much strength. Elias grabbed him by the front of his hoodie and squeezed. The boy continued to beat at Elias with his fist.

"Keep it up and I'll choke the life out of you. Got it?" His hand tightened even more and the boy gasped for breath and stopped struggling.

Wyatt ran up to them, breathing heavily. "You got him?"

"Yeah. You're a little out of breath there, Wyatt."

Wyatt slipped handcuffs on the boy, ignoring Elias, and led him back to the group without another word being said. In the darkness, it was hard to see expressions but Elias knew Wyatt was sending him one of his custom-made cold stares.

Elias trailed behind Wyatt and the kid, eager to see how this turned out. Stuart had handcuffs on the other

two boys still standing against the car. Wyatt led the kid back to his spot.

Looking at the boy closely, Wyatt said, "I don't believe I know you. Are you new in town?"

"None of your business," the boy spat.

Wyatt tapped his badge with the flashlight. "You see that? That means I'm the sheriff of this county and when you rob places and run from the law, it becomes my business. What's your name?"

"Get out of my face."

Elias had had enough of the kid's mouth. He needed an attitude adjustment. Before he could stop himself, he stepped in front of Wyatt and faced the kid. "You need to learn some manners and respect and if you don't, I'm going to teach them to you. When the sheriff asks you a question you say, 'yes, sir' or 'no, sir,' and when he asks you a direct question you answer it. Got it?"

A palpable heat emanated from the boy. And anger.

"You already know that I'm stronger than you, so give it up, kid. It's time to face the music."

The boy's stubborn expression reminded Elias of someone, but he couldn't place it. Invisible daggers from Wyatt pierced his back, so he stepped aside.

"What's your name?" Wyatt asked again.

The boy raised his head and stared at Elias. "My name is…Chase…McCray."

"I know all the McCray boys and you're not one of them," Wyatt pointed out.

"I'm not from here nor do I want to be a part of the McCrays. My mom and I moved here two weeks ago."

"Who's your mother?"

"Maribel McCray."

That got Elias's attention. This was the kid she'd been looking for—a wild teenager out of control.

"Read them their rights and take them to the jail!" Wyatt shouted to Stuart.

"It was all my idea," Chase said. "Don't punish them. It's all on me."

Wyatt placed his hands on his hips. "A few minutes ago you were willing to run away, leaving your friends holding the bag. Now you're trying to protect them?"

The kid glanced at Elias again and replied, "Yes…sir."

"Okay, we're going to the jail and we'll discuss this with your parents."

The boys had nothing to say.

"Call Bubba to tow this car," Wyatt called after Stuart.

"I'm on it."

Wyatt pulled off his hat and scratched his head, staring at Elias. "I'm trying to figure out what you're doing here, but then I know you and sometimes I wonder if you're ever going to grow up. I don't manhandle kids, Elias, and that was totally out of line."

The ruts on Wyatt's forehead were deep enough to hold molasses. But Wyatt's ire didn't faze Elias. He leaned against the patrol car. "Well, my daddy always taught me when you start a job, you finish it. And if I hadn't been here, that kid would be halfway to Temple by now."

"I would have caught him, Elias."

"Yeah, right."

Wyatt opened the back of the SUV. "Help me put this beer in the back of my car. Their parents will want to see the evidence."

"You're good at giving orders."

"Comes with the job."

"Uh-huh."

They stored the beer in Wyatt's back seat. "Do you know Maribel McCray?"

"Yeah. I went to high school with her. She was always snotty when I tried to talk to her."

Wyatt closed the back of the SUV. "How did you expect her to be? The Rebel/McCray feud was strong back then."

"True. She left town without even graduating. I guess she's finally come home."

"Do you know where she's living?"

"Now, Wyatt, the less I know about the McCrays, the better off I am."

Wyatt opened the driver's door of his car. "It's been peaceful lately with the McCrays marrying into the Rebel family. But I have a feeling this kid is going to stir it all up again."

Elias tapped Wyatt's badge with his finger. "You're the sheriff. You can handle it." With a smile, Elias walked through the woods to Rowdy's. He went inside and locked the back door. Bob came charging in, wiping his hands on his apron.

"Did Wyatt catch 'em?"

"Yes, he did. They're on their way to jail."

"Is it anybody I know?"

Elias told him about the boys.

Bob shook his hand. "What were they thinking?"

"The new kid in town is a bad influence."

"Maribel's boy?"

"Yeah. Do you still have her phone number?"

Bob hurried into the bar area and came back with the napkin. Elias slipped it into his pocket, and headed for the jail.

This time Maribel wasn't going to ignore him.

Chapter Two

Maribel rushed through the sheriff's door, a total wreck. She hadn't even bothered to comb her hair, which in hindsight she should have. It had a natural curl and seemed to be everywhere. Taking a deep breath, she tucked it behind her ears.

She'd been looking for Chase all night and had been unable to find him. She'd let him take her car and he'd promised to be home by ten o'clock. When he wasn't, Phoenix had let her borrow Rosie's truck. She'd searched all over town to no avail, and then the sheriff had called.

This was so unlike her son. He was a good kid, but she knew he was still angry about the move from Dallas. At seventeen, he thought the world revolved around him. That was her fault. She'd spoiled him. Her world was crumbling around her and she wasn't sure what to do next. First thing, she had to find a job because they couldn't continue to live with Rosie and Phoenix. Chase's disruptive behavior was causing problems and Maribel didn't want the stress to affect her sister, so she had to find a place for her and Chase. But she had bigger problems now.

She stepped into a small reception area that had a desk and filing cabinets, but no one was there. The hall opened into a big room. Two desks were empty and a deputy sat at another, writing in a folder. To the left, in a separate room,

was the sheriff's office. The nameplate on the open door said Wyatt Carson—Sheriff. He was a nice-looking man, probably in his early forties. She didn't remember him, but she remembered the Carson family.

With every ounce of courage she had left in her, she walked up to his desk, ignoring Elias, who was sitting in a chair. What was he doing here?

"Where's my son?" she blurted out.

The sheriff got to his feet and nodded toward a hall and she could see the bars of a jail cell. "He's in there."

Her breath caught in her throat, but she quickly straightened her back to regain her composure. Doing so, she realized she hadn't introduced herself. She held out her hand. "I'm Maribel McCray."

He shook her hand. "Wyatt Carson."

"What has he done?" She decided to go with patience and politeness instead of anger.

"He was arrested with two other boys for stealing beer from Rowdy's and two other places."

She shook her head. "No, you must have the wrong boy. My kid is—"

"—a good kid," he finished for her. "I've had two other parents tell me the same thing tonight, but I assure you, your son was involved. Actually, he confessed to being the ringleader."

Her stomach tied into a knot so tight she had trouble speaking. Chase was never in trouble. She licked her dry lips. "May I see him?"

The sheriff picked up a set of keys from his desk. "Sure, but leave your purse here."

She placed her purse on the desk, fully aware that Elias was watching her every move. It surprised her that he wasn't saying anything. Elias always had an opinion. She followed the sheriff, continuing to ignore Elias, which

was her normal reaction when she saw him. Her shoulders burned from his sharp gaze.

The sheriff unlocked the steel doors and they banged with a chilling sound. Goose bumps popped up on her arms. There were two cots in the room and that was it. Chase lay on one of them. When he saw her, he jumped to his feet, his eyes bracketed with fear. Her heart squeezed at the sight. Where had she gone wrong?

When the sheriff walked away, she sat on the bunk and Chase sat beside her. "I'm sorry, Mom."

Words rolled around in her head like loose marbles and she couldn't pull them together to complete a sentence. She'd never been this scared in her whole life, not even when she'd been seventeen and pregnant. An angel had been watching over her and had delivered her into the hands of Mrs. Lavinia Wainwright, otherwise known as Miss Vennie—but she was Nana to her and Chase.

When her dad had discovered she was pregnant, he'd kicked her out of the house. Her mother had wrung her hands and cried, but never lifted a finger to help her. Instead, she'd shoved money into her hand and had told her to go to Mrs. Peabody's, an elderly lady in town who rented rooms. But Maribel knew she couldn't stay in Horseshoe, listening to the gossip and the rumors.

Mrs. Peabody had sent her to Dallas to stay with her sister, Miss Vennie. That was the luckiest day of Maribel's life, except for the day Chase was born. Miss Vennie had a big house in Dallas and she had accepted Maribel with open arms. Maribel had learned about love and trust and family and she'd found a home like she'd never had before.

Miss Vennie had treated Chase as if he were her own son. While Maribel had worked, Miss Vennie had taken care of Chase and Maribel hadn't needed to worry about him. For years they'd had a good life. Then Miss Vennie

had died and Maribel's whole world had come apart once again. They had to move out of the house because it was mortgaged to the hilt. She'd rented an apartment and everything had been going smoothly until she'd lost her job. She'd been scrambling, looking for work when Rosie had called and she knew then it was time to go home. Now she was wondering if that had been the right decision.

"Mom, aren't you going to say anything? I know you're disappointed in me…"

Words suddenly filled her throat. "Yes, I'm very disappointed in you. Where's my kid? I don't know this kid who steals beer. My kid sat by Nana's bedside and read her Bible verses to comfort her in her last days. My kid served food during the holidays at the homeless shelter. That's my kid." She looked around the dismal cinder block cell. "I don't know this kid behind bars."

"I'm sorry, Mom. I want to go home to Dallas. I don't like it here."

"Is that what this is all about? You think you can manipulate me into moving back to Dallas?"

Chase hung his head.

"We can't go back. There's nothing left for us there. I couldn't find a job, which means I have to find work here, and you're not making it easy for us. I'll have to use some of the money I saved to get you out of here."

Chase's eyes grew round. "You mean the sheriff is thinking of keeping me in here?"

"Yes. Stealing is against the law. I thought my straight-A student son would know that."

"Mom, I didn't hurt anybody."

She was aghast at his attitude. "Is that how you look at it? Well, you did hurt someone. You hurt Bob, the owner of Rowdy's. That's how he makes his living, selling beer, and when you stole from him, it cut into his profits."

"I just want to go home to Dallas and my old school in August. I'm a good football player and no one is going to notice me here in this small town. I won't get recruited and I won't get to play in the NFL. That's been my goal my whole life and now it's all ruined. How could you bring us here?"

She took a deep breath, trying to think of words that would get through to him. "Young guys with a record don't get recruited, either."

"What?"

"I told you stealing is a crime and it will go on your record if I can't get it removed."

"Mom, you have to do something."

"You know, Chase, you're seventeen years old and it's time you started acting like it instead of a spoiled little boy."

"If you get me out of here, I promise to do better. I just…"

"I know. You don't like it here. But in life you don't get everything you like. Right now, my main concern is putting food in our mouths and a roof over our heads. That's what's important, Chase. We have to move out of Phoenix's house because of your disruptive behavior. And I wanted to be there for my sister."

"They don't like me."

"Have you given them a chance? Instead of being moody, you could offer to help every now and then. And you could play with Jake."

Chase frowned. "He's a baby."

"So? It's called helping out and being glad someone took us in." She got to her feet. "I have to sort this mess out." She looked at him with his hunched shoulders and that frown etched on his face. It seemed to be permanent.

"You know who else would be disappointed to see you in this cell?"

He buried his face in his hands. "Nana," he mumbled.

"Yes, think about that." Maribel walked to the steel bars and a deputy opened it for her. With more enthusiasm than she was feeling she went straight to the sheriff's office. Elias was still sitting in the chair and she ignored him as best as she could.

"What do I have to do to get my son out of jail?"

The sheriff leaned back in his chair. "Miss McCray, I'm not inclined to do that."

She curled one hand into a fist. "Why not? I didn't see the other boys in there so you must have let them go. Why is my boy different?"

"When we caught them, your boy ran. The others didn't."

What! She tried not to let the shock show on her face but she feared she'd failed. She was at a loss at what to do, but she couldn't leave her son in jail. There had to be a way.

She bit her lip. "Don't you usually set bail?"

The sheriff leaned forward. "Usually. Ralph, the bail bondsman, is next door but he's asleep at home at this hour and I don't feel obligated to call him. I think a night in jail might help your son realize how serious his actions were."

"Please." Begging was not in her nature, but at this point she had no other choice.

"Okay." He opened a drawer and pulled out a ledger. "I can set bail. I do that a lot, small town and all, and that keeps Ralph from trudging up here in the middle of the night."

"Thank you."

"A thousand dollars should guarantee that he doesn't run and that he'll be at the hearing on Monday. And it should cover everything they've stolen."

A ball of fear wedged inside her chest. "I can't afford that. Can't you just release him into my custody? I'll make sure he stays in line and I won't let him have the car anymore."

"Normally I would do that, but you see, I don't know you or your son. I could release him into your care and in no time you could be out of state and the other two boys would take the fall for the crime."

"I wouldn't do that. My sister is here and I wouldn't leave her, either."

"I'm sorry, Miss McCray, but that's the deal. Your boy has an attitude and a sarcastic mouth. He needs to learn a lesson and he needs to learn it now. That's just my advice to you."

He wasn't going to relent. There was no way she could leave her son in jail. Yes, he deserved it. But she was a mother and a mother always fought for her kid, no matter what. Which meant she would have to do something now she'd sworn she would never do.

There was a saying about paying the piper. She had never quite understood what that meant, but suddenly she did. She would now have to pay for everything that had happened in the last seventeen years and she would have to pay with her pride.

She sucked air into her tight chest and turned to Elias. "Can I see you outside for a minute?" Without waiting for an answer, she walked confidently toward the receptionist's desk. Behind her she could hear:

"Was she talking to me?" Elias asked.

"I think she was," the sheriff replied.

She paused long enough to make sure Elias was following her. She went through the door and the warm June breeze kissed the heat of her cheeks. A faint hum of traffic from the interstate broke the early morning silence. Fading

moonlight and the ancient streetlights provided illumination. She walked toward one of the old live oak trees that shaded the courthouse, and sat on the bench beneath it.

Words rolled around in her head again and she desperately searched for the right ones to start the conversation. It wouldn't be easy, but nothing in life for her had been.

Elias sat beside her and she wanted to move away. He was too close for her comfort zone. In high school, they were always looking at each other, but they both knew that's all they could do. With their feuding families, there was no way they could ever go out on a date or even socialize. That's just the way it was. But she had always thought he was the most handsome guy in school. Tall and lanky with an attitude that bespoke confidence, he had a daredevil approach to life that had been exciting for a young girl.

Nothing was said for a few seconds. "You wanted to talk, so talk," he said. "But before you start, I just want you to know I'm not loaning you any money."

"Elias, I need help, and I'll pay you back."

"Do you have a job?"

She forced herself not to fidget. "No, not yet, but I will soon."

"I'm not in the habit of loaning people money, especially if they don't have a job. And for the record, Wyatt was right. Your kid needs to learn a lesson."

"You don't even know my kid."

"I think I do. I'm the one who tackled him when he ran off."

"You did what?"

"He ran, Maribel, from the law, and they will stick him good for that."

She turned on the seat to face him, not caring how close she was. "You can't let that happen. His whole future is

ahead of him. He made a mistake because he's upset about the move from Dallas. You see, he's a good football player and he wants to play in the NFL. He thinks all his dreams have been ruined because he won't be playing for a big school. Instead, he'll be playing here in Horseshoe. He's mad and that's my fault. I shouldn't have uprooted him."

"So the stealing thing was his stupid attempt to get you to move back to Dallas?"

"Yes."

He rested his forearms on his knees and clasped his hands. "I don't understand why you're telling me this or asking me for money. You have family here and I should be the last person you'd ask since you wouldn't even speak to me earlier at Rowdy's, just like in high school."

"Things had to be that way in high school."

He rubbed his hands together. "I know."

"I can't ask my family. None of them have tried to make contact since I've been home and I can't ask Phoenix and Rosie. They have their own problems right now and I don't want to cause them any extra worry."

"But why me?"

She kept talking because she didn't want to answer that question and with luck she wouldn't have to. "I have an interview with Gladys at the diner and I feel sure she's going to hire me."

"For minimum wage?"

"Yes, but it's a start."

"What did you do in Dallas?"

"At first, waitress. Then after I got my high school diploma, I attended a junior college and took restaurant management courses. That enabled me to get a better job and I worked my way up the ladder to being a manager of an upscale restaurant. I can start over again and I can pay you so much each week."

"I could be married, Maribel. Have you ever thought of that? My wife wouldn't like me throwing my money away, and investing in your kid is like throwing money away."

"You're not married," she stated with confidence.

"How do you know that?"

"Because no one would marry you."

"Really? Is that the way you talk to a man you're asking for money from?"

"You're wild and crazy, Elias, and everyone knows it. There's not a woman in this town who could tame you."

"You got that right."

"Remember that time you brought beer to school and Bubba and another boy got drunk and you tried to jump off the roof as a superhero? Someone told the principal and he came out and told you to get off the roof. You jumped and fell right on him."

"My shirt wasn't a very good cape."

"See, young guys do crazy things and that's what Chase is doing now. I just need your help to get him out of this so he won't have a record. Please, Elias." Begging was getting easier, especially when it concerned her son.

He rested against the back of the bench and stretched out his long legs. "Give me a good reason I should loan you money."

"I'll pay you back. Why do I have to give you a reason? Just call it—"

He wagged a finger in her face. "Don't call it a *friend* thing because we were never friends."

"Why do you have to be so…?"

"Crazy?"

"Yes. Why can't you just help me? Do something good for a change."

"Give me a reason, Maribel. A very good reason to part with my money."

They were going around in circles and she was growing weary. He wanted a reason and she could give him a good one, but it would take a slice of her pride just like she'd known in the sheriff's office. She would have to say the words out loud for the first time in her life. She would have to say them to Elias. There was no other way.

Her stomach cramped tight. "You want a reason? I'll give you one."

"Let's hear it."

The words stuck in her throat. She swallowed, trying to force them out. But they were trapped in the mind of that seventeen-year-old girl who had run instead of facing the gossip and the rumors and a man she barely knew. Life had come full circle and she had to say the words she should've said years ago.

"You're…his father."

Chapter Three

Elias laughed so hard it startled the pigeons roosting on the top of the courthouse. "Wow, Maribel, you had to reach deep for that one."

"It's true."

He shook his head. "No way am I that kid's father. You're not going to pull that on me."

"Are you losing your memory, Elias?"

"No, my memory is fine, thank you."

"Then you'll remember that evening in February when I had a flat tire and you stopped to help me. It was drizzling rain and it started to sleet and you suggested we get in your truck until it let up. Remember that?"

Every day of my life since.

He shifted uncomfortably on the bench. "One time, Maribel, and we used a condom. So you can stop right now."

"Condoms don't work all the time."

Elias remembered when his brother Phoenix had received the news that he was the father of a two-year-old boy. Phoenix had been surprised because he'd said they'd used a condom, but Jake was very much alive and Phoenix's. No, no, no, she wasn't going to pull this on him. No way was that kid his. He would know, wouldn't he? The doubts circled like buzzards and they began to peck at his brain. He didn't like that. He was happy with his life and

he didn't need all this drama. She was a McCray and she was yanking his chain. That had to be the explanation. She just wanted him to pay the fine.

"That was in early February and you didn't leave town until late April. You obviously slept with someone else in the intervening time."

"Have you really looked at Chase?"

"What?"

"Go look at him, Elias, and come back and tell me he's not your son. And I won't say another word."

She was playing him like a pro but he wasn't falling for it. "There's no need for me to look at him."

"Are you scared?"

"No. He's not my kid."

"Then go look at him. If he's not yours, what are you afraid of?"

He got to his feet, knowing there was only one way to make her stop with all the nonsense. "Okay, and this will be the end of it."

"Yes."

As he walked back into the sheriff's office, the air held a faint moistness from the early morning dew. Where had the night gone? He should be crawling out of bed, getting ready with his brothers for another day of baling and hauling hay. Yet, here he was, stuck in a nightmare.

He and Maribel had always liked each other and that night in February, sitting in his truck, things had gotten out of control. And not just him. They both had experienced something they didn't want to talk about or admit out loud, so they didn't. Afterward, they'd decided they would never see or talk to each other again. It was mutual. It was over. And now… There was just no way.

Wyatt noticed him walking toward the cells. "Elias, what are you doing?"

"Just give me a minute."

"I'm ready to go home and I don't have time to deal with all this nonsense."

"Just a minute, Wyatt."

Elias stopped in front of the cell and Chase jumped up from the cot. "What do you want?"

Elias stared at the kid, the dark hair, the dark eyes and the lean, lanky frame. He took a couple steps backward as the truth hit him like a sucker punch, almost bringing him to his knees. It was like looking in a mirror when he was that age. All that arrogance, all that anger and all that resentment was him back then. It took the strong hand of his father to turn him around and even then Elias had fought him all the way. He saw all that in the eyes of the kid staring back at him. Oh, man!

For some reason he pulled out his phone and took a step toward the cell. He stuck his arm through the bars and snapped a picture of Chase's face.

"What are you doing? You can't take a picture of me. That has to be illegal and you need my permission."

"Give it a rest, kid."

Wyatt grabbed Elias's arm and pulled him away. "What are you doing?"

"I'm not sure, but you better stick around because I'm going back outside and I just might kill Maribel McCray."

"Elias…"

Elias hit the door at full speed and didn't even pause when Wyatt called again. He went straight to Maribel with fire in his belly. "I could strangle the life right out of you and I still might. How could you keep something like that from me? And don't say it was because I'm a Rebel. That's not gonna wash."

"I tried," came out low, but he heard it.

"How? And when?"

"I was sick in the mornings and my dad figured out I was pregnant. He demanded to know who the father was. I wouldn't tell him. If I had, he would have killed you. He took out his belt and beat me with it, insisting that I tell him. When he realized I wasn't going to, he told me to get out of the house and to never come back. He called me a slut."

Some of the anger eased from Elias as he started to see the past from her point of view. His parents had never hit them and he couldn't imagine what it must have been like for a young girl to be hit time and time again.

"I got in my truck and drove away. I paid for the truck myself from working at the bakery so he couldn't take that away from me. I didn't know where to go or what to do, but as I was leaving my mom shoved three hundred dollars in my hand and told me to go to Mrs. Peabody's."

Elias sat on the bench beside her as she continued to talk. "As I was driving away, I thought I wasn't the only one who had created this baby and you needed to know you were going to be a father. I went to Rebel Ranch to find you."

Elias sat up straight. "You went to the ranch?"

"Yes. Your grandfather answered the door and when he saw me he called for your mother. The moment she saw me she demanded to know what I wanted. I told her I wanted to see Elias and she told me I wasn't seeing her son." Maribel wiped at her face.

Was she crying? Oh, no. He couldn't stand it when women cried. He just held his breath and waited for more because he knew there was no way his mother would have turned away a Rebel grandchild.

"She then asked me why I wanted to see you and I had no choice. I had to tell her. I hoped she'd let me see you then, but that hope was short-lived. She said, 'Get out of

my house and if you spread that rumor around Horseshoe, I will have you arrested.'"

"Nah." Elias shook his head. "You had me up until then. My mom wouldn't do that. I know that beyond any doubt."

"I'm not lying, Elias. Ask your grandfather. He was there. He even said, 'Kate, you need to listen to the girl.' She told him to shut up and that was it. I ran to my truck and drove straight to Mrs. Peabody's. I told Mrs. Peabody I had nowhere to go. She said she would find me a place away from Horseshoe. She called her sister in Dallas who said I could stay with her until I got on my feet. I went to the bakery and picked up my paycheck and told Doris I wouldn't be coming back. I drove away, leaving everything behind—the heartache, the pain and my family."

Elias rubbed his hands together, trying to believe what she was saying. His mother's part in this he didn't believe, just yet. It didn't ring true for the woman he knew, the mother who always stood up for her children and fought for them. He'd deal with that later. Right now, he was grappling with the fact that he had a child, an out-of-control son.

"I'll pay you back, Elias. I just can't let my son stay in jail."

Elias got to his feet. "I'm not spending one dime to get that kid out of jail." He headed back to the sheriff's office with Maribel behind him.

"You don't mean that!"

She followed him straight into the sheriff's office. "Elias, please."

"I need to talk to you, Wyatt."

"Elias." Wyatt sighed. "It's five o'clock in the morning. I'm going home and whatever you want to talk about we can do it on Monday."

"We have to do it now."

Wyatt stared right at him. "Why?"

"You asked me for a favor and now I'm asking you for one."

Wyatt laid down the pen he was holding. "I'm almost afraid to ask, but what favor?"

"I want you to release Chase McCray into my custody without any money changing hands."

Wyatt gave a chuckle. "I think you're sleep deprived. I'm not releasing Chase McCray to anyone. He stays in jail."

"You released the other two boys into the custody of their parents."

"Yes, because I know them and I know they'll be in court on Monday morning."

"You know me, too, don't you, Wyatt?"

"Too well. And I know once you get something in your mind you never let it go, just like an old hound dog."

"So you know I'm not stopping until you release him into my custody."

Wyatt sighed again. "Elias, why is this kid so important to you?"

He took a deep breath and said the words for the first time: "He's my son."

"What?" Wyatt frowned and looked from Elias to Maribel. "You mean you and Maribel were a thing in high school?"

"Yes. It happened one time and we both knew that because of our families we couldn't be together and we never saw each other again. I didn't know Maribel was pregnant and she told me for the first time tonight. So, are you going to let my kid go or not?"

Wyatt ran his hands through his hair. "Holy cow. This is just what I need. I knew something was going on with

this kid and now the Rebel/McCray feud is going to get stirred up all over again."

"You don't have to worry about Chase running. I'll stick to him like butter on a biscuit. I'll have him at the courthouse on time for the hearing. And you know I always keep my word."

"I just can't release someone because you ask me to."

Elias leaned over and tapped Wyatt's badge on his khaki shirt. "You're the sheriff and you can do anything you want. I've seen you do it many times and no one has questioned you. The people in this community trust you to make the right decisions."

Wyatt reached for the keys. "Damn it! I'm going to release him into your custody and if he does one little thing and is not there for the hearing—" Wyatt pointed to the jail cell "—you'll be sitting in that cell."

"Got it." Elias took the keys from Wyatt. "I want to talk to him first."

"No," Maribel spoke up. "I'll tell him. He needs to hear it from me."

Elias faced the woman who'd just driven an ice pick through his heart. "I will tell him. You had the opportunity for seventeen years and now it's my turn. He needs to hear this from me—his father."

"I need to do this," Maribel insisted.

He shook his head. "Not gonna happen. That kid has an attitude and he's going to learn respect and manners and he's going to learn it from me."

Wyatt coughed.

Elias looked at his friend. "You think I can't do it?"

"I just want to go home. Whatever you do with your child is your business. But I'll say one thing for you, Elias. You've always shown me respect, even when you were in the wrong."

"Elias…" Maribel called after him as he walked away to the cell. Chase lay on the cot with his hands behind his head. He slowly sat up when he saw Elias entering the cell.

"What do you want?"

Elias sat on a cot, facing his son and he couldn't stop staring at him and reliving the memories that churned inside him. That night when he had come upon Maribel fixing a flat, he thought all his prayers had been answered. There had been an electricity between them for some time and he had just wanted to talk to her, away from school, away from their families. She'd accepted his help graciously and then they had scrambled into his truck to get away from the sleet.

Breathing the same air as Maribel had been as intoxicating as any beer he'd ever had. She'd smelled of strawberries, and being young and stupid and besotted he'd thought it was because of her strawberry colored hair. He'd loved being close to her. Her hair had been wet and he'd grabbed an old jacket from the back seat and had helped to rub it dry. When he'd touched her skin, her soft skin, something had happened to both of them and they'd kept on touching each other. One kiss had led to another and before either of them could stop, they were ripping off clothes and getting warm in an old familiar way.

She was the sexiest girl he'd ever touched. He remembered every emotion he had felt that night. It was like a movie in his head and he could bring it up at the oddest of times. Her moans, her smile, her long hair all around him. He remembered it almost every day of his life. And he regretted it almost every day of his life. Now, he was staring at the results of that night. The child they'd created, not in love but in passion. A powerful passion. And after it was gone, the only thing that had remained was the regrets.

"Are you just gonna stare at me, or what?"

"What has your mother told you about your father?"

"What? That's none of your business."

"You know we had this talk about manners and respect. Do we need to have it again?"

Chase frowned. "Are you a deputy, or what?"

"Or what."

"Why do you want to know about my dad?"

"I'm just curious. Your mom is trying to get you out of jail and…"

Chase tried to see around the bars. "Is she talking to the sheriff?"

"Yes, he wants a thousand dollars upfront to make sure you don't run or leave town."

"My mom doesn't have that kind of money."

"Maybe your dad does."

"I don't know who he is. Mom doesn't talk about him. The only thing she told me was that he was someone in high school, someone she shouldn't have gotten involved with. He wasn't ready to be a father and she had to raise me alone. She never told him about me, and that's okay. We had Nana."

"Who's Nana?"

"She's my grandmother, or the lady who took my mother in when she was pregnant. She became my grandmother and she loved both of us. It hasn't been the same since she died. After that, we had to move into an apartment. We did okay until Mom's boss fired her because she wouldn't sleep with him."

Maribel had failed to mention that. He could imagine her life must've been pretty hard raising the kid alone. He was glad she'd had someone there for her like Nana to help. The guilt was now beating against his head with the force of a two-by-four. He should have known something was wrong when she'd left town without graduat-

ing. He should've been the one to put it together, but he had been busy doing other things. Maturity hadn't been his strong suit back then, and some people would say it wasn't now, either.

Elias decided to let it go for now. Later, he and Maribel would talk about a lot of things. He rested his forearms on his thighs and looked at his son. "You seem to have had a pretty good life. Why are you so angry?"

Chase looked down at the floor. "I don't like it here. No one wants us here. I want to go back home to Dallas. I play football and I'm hoping scouts will notice me and I can get a scholarship to college because Mom won't be able to afford to pay for me to go. I want to play in the NFL. All that is ruined now and I'll never get noticed in this one-horse town. My life is over."

"So life is all about you. Have you even thought about what it's like for your mother to come back here and face her family and the guy who is your father?"

"No." Chase continued to look at the floor.

"Have you ever thought of getting a job to help out?"

His head jerked up. "A job? I don't know how to do anything except play football."

"That's going to change."

Chase narrowed his eyes. "Says who?"

"Says me. You have to pay for the beer you stole and to do that you have to get a job and make money. A new concept, huh?"

"My mom will pay for it."

Elias's shook his head. "No. You will, and I'm going to make sure that you do."

"You can't make me do anything. My mom won't let you."

The crux of all Chase's problems—his mother. Elias was going to undo some of that, at least the pampering.

"You're seventeen years old and it's time for you to stand up and be a man and take responsibility for what you did."

"I'm sorry, okay?" There was a note of regret in his voice and it was the first sign that it was getting harder to carry around that big ol' attitude.

Elias got to his feet. "The sheriff has released you into my custody."

"What? Why would he do that? I don't even know you. My mother will not stand for this."

"Your mother has agreed, so this discussion is over."

"I'm not going with you. I'd rather stay in jail."

Elias placed his hands on his hips and stared at this kid that he and Maribel had created. It was time for a dose of reality. For the kid. And for Elias. "That guy from high school who your mom said wasn't ready for responsibility would have taken full responsibility for you."

"How do you know that?"

"I'm that guy. I'm your father."

Chapter Four

"No." Chase shook his head. "You're not my father. My mom would've told me."

"She told me for the first time tonight, so I'm in shock just like you. I guess she never wanted either one of us to know."

Maribel couldn't stand it any longer. She walked to the open jail door and faced her son. They rarely talked about Chase's father and she liked it that way. But now her pride was going to take another hit. She had never meant to keep it a secret. It had just happened. Never in a million years had she planned to tell Chase this way.

"Mom, tell him it's not true. He's not my father." Chase was not ready to hear the truth, but he was mature enough to handle it. If he wasn't, that was her fault.

She stepped closer to Chase and spoke softly. "Elias Rebel is your father. I'm sorry. I should've told you more about him, but I didn't feel it was necessary at the time. I never planned to return to Horseshoe."

A shattered look came over his face. She'd seen that same look the day Miss Vennie had died. A part of her would hurt the rest of her life for creating this moment—for hurting her son like this.

Chase jerked a thumb toward Elias. "He says the sher-

iff released me into his custody and I'm now his responsibility."

Maribel was tired and didn't want to deal with more drama tonight. "We'll discuss this later." She nodded toward the doorway. "Let's go home."

Chase followed her without another word. Maribel was very aware that Elias was behind them. She had to make a stand and she had to do it now. Stepping outside in the early morning dawn, she turned to face Elias and all her sins seemed to hit her full force. His stern expression sent a direct message to her heart: he wasn't going to go quietly out of their lives. Her stomach roiled with anxiety. But maybe he just needed a nudge.

"I really appreciated your help tonight. You went above and beyond what I expected and I'm very grateful my son did not have to spend more time in jail, but I can take it from here. I will make sure he's at the hearing on Monday and he will be grounded until this is over."

"Really, Maribel? You think I'm going to slither out of my son's life with gratitude?"

"I'm not your son!" Chase shouted.

Elias's lips tightened and she could see it was an effort to control his temper. "This is how it's going to go," he stated, his voice clear and unrelenting. "You take the kid back to Phoenix's and get some rest. I'll follow you out to Rebel Road and then I have to talk to my mom and my brothers to let them know what has happened."

She should be thankful he was willing to take responsibility but she didn't need his help now. All she wanted was for him to disappear out of their lives once again. She had raised Chase all these years and she could continue to do so without his input. She was fighting for her independence and somehow she knew it would be the biggest fight of her life.

"There's really no need…"

"What are you afraid of, Maribel?" An eyebrow lifted toward his hat. "Are you afraid my mother might tell a different story than you've told me?"

"I'm not afraid. I know the truth, but there's no need to rehash the past. It's over and we should all move on."

"Yeah, we'll see," he said in a snarky tone that irritated her. She'd had enough for tonight and walked toward Rosie's truck and got in. Chase followed. Nothing else was said as Elias went to his truck. All the way to Rebel Road she was aware of his truck behind her. He wasn't letting them out of his sight. When she passed the Rebel Ranch house, he turned into the entrance and Maribel breathed a sigh of relief.

She had to wonder how his meeting with his mother would go. She wasn't going to take it well. Since Maribel had been living with Phoenix and Rosie, Miss Kate had avoided her, but she couldn't avoid her son. He would want answers. She'd love to be a fly on that wall. But then again, she'd rather forget the whole thing. She had a permanent reminder, though, who stalked behind her into the house.

"Go to bed," she said to her son. "We'll talk when you get up."

"Mom…"

Phoenix came into the kitchen where they were standing. "You're home. I have to get to work."

Chase walked passed Phoenix without saying a word in his usual sullen mood.

"What happened?" Phoenix asked, staring at Chase's back.

She told him most of what had happened during the night. She didn't mention Elias, but Phoenix had to know and Rosie did, too.

"He's out of control, Maribel. You have to do something."

She took a deep breath. "I know. You've never asked me who Chase's father is and neither has Rosie."

"I figured that was your business."

"Yes, well, to get Chase out of jail I had to ask for his father's help, so this whole town will know by the end of today. I want to tell Rosie and I need your permission to do that."

"Who's his father?"

Her throat went dry and she had to swallow to say the words. "Your...brother...Elias."

"What!"

"It's true. It was a one-time thing that should never have happened. Chase is a result of that one time. I never told Elias but I had to tell him tonight because I needed his help."

Phoenix swiped a hand through his hair. "Oh, man. Does my mother know about this?"

"Elias is telling her now." She didn't elaborate. She'd let Elias tell them the rest.

Phoenix grabbed his hat from a rack near the door. "Rosie and Jake are still asleep. Do you mind fixing breakfast?"

"No. Can I tell Rosie? I wouldn't want her to hear it from someone else."

"Sure." He walked out the door and Maribel trailed down the hall to the master bedroom. Rosie, with her red hair everywhere, was propped up against the headboard. When she was small, Maribel had called her "Little Red Hen" because of her hair. They'd had an old hen that had had feathers the same color.

"You're awake."

"I always wake up when Phoenix kisses me goodbye."

Maribel sat at the foot of the bed. "You're absolutely glowing."

Placing her hand on her protruding stomach, Rosie said, "I can't lose this baby."

"You're won't because we're not going to let you. You have about three months to wait and even if the baby comes early, she'll still be okay."

"Phoenix and I are happy it's a girl. We're going to call her Grace. Gracie for short."

"And she'll be beautiful just like her mother."

Rosie frowned. "Are you just getting home? You had those clothes on yesterday."

She told her sister about the events of the night and ended by saying, "I had to ask his father for help."

Rosie leaned forward. "His father!"

She met her sister's startled eyes. "You've never asked me about him."

"I didn't want to pry and I knew you would tell me when you were ready." She paused for a second. "So… who is Chase's father?"

"Elias."

"Elias who?"

"Rosie…"

"Oh…you mean…Elias Rebel?"

"Yes."

Rosie shook her head. "I don't see how that could have happened. You never went out at night or dated."

Maribel told her the whole story and Rosie crawled to the foot of the bed and sat by Maribel. "I was so scared and I didn't know what to do when Miss Kate wouldn't believe me."

Rosie hugged her sister. "With everything that was going on at that time I guess it's understandable that she wouldn't. But still…it makes me sad."

"I hope Elias doesn't get into a big argument with his mom about it."

"Elias can handle his mother. I don't think I know anyone stronger than Elias. He's rough around the edges and as tough as they come."

"And handsome," slipped out before Maribel could stop herself.

Rosie picked up on it immediately. "Oh, do you still have feelings for him?"

"Of course not." The words sounded hollow to her own ears and she decided to be honest with her sister. "I thought I was in love with him. Being a silly teenager, it was clear to me that after we had sex, we'd run away and live happily ever after. That naive teenager woke up quickly. It was just wrong and we both knew it, except for one little thing. I was pregnant."

Rosie hugged her again. "Oh, Mari, I'm sorry for all that you had to go through."

Another person called her Mari, but he pronounced it Merry. Sometimes late at night she'd hear his voice in her head and she hated that she couldn't forget it. That she couldn't forget him.

Maribel hugged her back. "I'm sorry I wasn't here to help you when you needed someone." She brushed Rosie's hair from her face. "Do you sometimes resent our mother for not helping us?"

"I did for a while, but I know she did the best she could."

"Every day our mother would say, 'I love you,' over and over, but it had no meaning when it counted. When Dad would hit us, she would just cry and wring her hands. Not once did she try to stop him and not once did she take up for us. The day he found out I was pregnant he hit me so hard I fell against the wall. I was afraid I was going to lose the baby. I grabbed my stomach, trying to protect it, and

I knew in that moment that I wanted the baby. I guess I'll always remember Mom standing there with tears in her eyes, wringing her hands and not lifting a finger to help me. I stopped believing in love that day. As I drove away, something inside me died. Later, I knew what it was—my ability to love."

"Oh, Mari."

"I would protect Chase with my dying breath if someone was trying to hurt him."

"Mom gave you money, as she did me. Doesn't that count for something? She tried to help in her own way. She was just weak and didn't know what else to do."

"No, it doesn't mean a thing. Shoving me off on Mrs. Peabody was not a motherly thing to do, even though it probably saved my life."

"You can't say that you don't feel love. You love Chase. You love me."

"Yeah, but I'll never say those words to anyone again. They're meaningless. That's the way I feel now and I can't change it."

"That's not healthy."

"Mama. Mama. Mama," Jake called as he ran into the room in his pajamas. "I'm hungry."

Rosie kissed her son. "Aunt Maribel will fix you something."

"'Kay."

Maribel took the boy's hand. "Come on, hotshot. Let's see what we can find for breakfast." Jake was almost four and he would be going to school in the fall. Rosie would have her hands full with a child in school and one in her arms. That was Rosie's life—the one she wanted, filled with all the happiness she deserved. It wasn't for Maribel. Maybe she was jaded. Or just smart. She would never get hurt again, though.

As she poured milk into a glass, she wondered what was happening at Rebel Ranch.

ELIAS SAT IN his truck outside his mom's house, trying to come to grips with everything that had happened during the night. He had a son. He and Maribel had a son. Fast on that thought came one that he had to deal with: Did his mother know? There was just no way she would deny a Rebel grandchild. The only way to find out the truth was to walk into the house and ask her, which would probably be the hardest thing he'd ever had to do besides burying his dad.

Phoenix drove up and ran into the house, not even noticing Elias in his truck.

Showtime, he thought, as he got out and made his way into the house. A ball of dread wedged in his throat. Most people thought that was an alien emotion to him. He felt fear just like everyone else, even though everyone called him tough as leather. Today, he would find out how tough he really was.

Everyone, even Grandpa, was sitting around the big kitchen table eating breakfast. His mom sat at the head of the table and he could see her clearly, making sure everyone had enough food, making sure her sons were well-fed before a long day's work.

Grandpa noticed him first. "Where have you been? You usually call when you're gonna stay out all night."

"Sorry, Grandpa, I didn't have time."

"You've been out all night and you plan to work today?" Falcon joined the conversation. "I hope you got some sleep along the way."

"No, I didn't get a wink."

"You look strange," Quincy added. "What's wrong with you?"

"I spent most of the night in Wyatt's office." He wasn't sure how to start the conversation so he started with the basics.

"Did you get arrested?" his mother asked.

"No. It's a long story so I'll try to shorten it as much as I can." He told them about the stolen beer and the kids and Maribel's son. "I went to the jail with Wyatt because I wanted to see what was going to happen to the boys. He let Billy Tom and Brandon go with their parents on the condition that they would be there for the hearing on Monday. And since he doesn't know Maribel, he was going to hold her son until the hearing. Maribel asked for my help and I told her she'd have to give me a good reason to help her keep her son out of jail. She gave me one I wasn't expecting." He looked directly at his mother. "She said Chase was my son."

"What!" echoed around the room.

Grandpa pointed a finger at Elias's mother. "I told you it was going to bite you in the butt one day."

"Shut up, Abe."

All his hopes that Maribel had somehow exaggerated the situation died in that moment. His mother had rejected his child. That left a bitter taste in his mouth. All his life he had looked up to his mother. She was rock solid with family loyalty and love. How could she have done this?

"I guess that answers my next question. Maribel did come here to find me. What did you say to her?"

His mother clamped her lips tight in indignation.

"I'll tell you what she said." Grandpa was eager to take up the story. "She said to get out of her house and if Maribel spread that lie around Horseshoe she would call the sheriff."

His mother got to her feet, her face a mask of fury. "The child is not yours, Elias. She's playing you. I thought you,

of all people, would see that. When she came here with that story, I told her my son would not betray his family. And he didn't. I know him."

Betrayal. Was that how she saw it?

His stomach hurt as if someone had tightened barbed wire around it. But he had to face the truth and he had to face his mother.

"I'm sorry if you see it as betrayal. It was two teenagers with raging hormones. It was a one-time thing and we knew it was wrong and we never saw each other again. We used protection but she still got pregnant and I never knew until tonight. I would have known if you had seen fit to tell me."

"That child is not yours. How many times do I have to tell you?"

Elias pulled out his phone, tapped the screen and walked over and laid Chase's picture in front of her. She refused to look at it. Falcon picked up the phone and stared at it.

"Oh…"

Quincy took it from him and passed it around the table. "Mom…"

"That is not Elias's son, Quincy."

"Mom…"

"Stay out of this, Phoenix."

"Maybe you need to get a DNA test done," Falcon suggested.

"I don't need a DNA test. I know Chase is my son."

"He is not your son, Elias," his mother repeated in a steely voice he'd never heard before. And it brought out the anger in him.

"What is it? Is it because he's *my* son? Falcon and Leah got pregnant and you and Dad then invited them into the house to live. When Leah left, you helped with the baby. There was no question of DNA. When Jude got Paige preg-

nant in high school and gave the child up for adoption, you hired an attorney to fight to get him back. There was no question of DNA then either. Phoenix heard he was a father and you wanted to raise the boy. So what is it? Why is my son treated differently?"

His mother carried her plate to the sink. "I'm tired of talking about this. We have work to do and it's time we all got to it."

Elias picked up his phone from the table. "That's it, huh? If my son is not welcome here then I'm not, either. I'm out of here."

"If you walk out that door, I will disinherit you."

A powerful silence filled the room.

He turned back to look at the mother he'd loved all his life and he only saw an angry woman determined to stick to her principles of being right when she was wrong. She didn't want to admit she'd made a mistake in turning away Elias's child. He couldn't change that, but he wasn't going to stand for it, either.

All his life he'd put his blood, sweat and tears into this ranch because one day he would own part of it. Could he walk away from everything he loved? It wasn't much of a choice. He had a son and he had to stand up for him as well as for himself. As always, though, he had something to say.

"Dad was alive back then. Don't you think a Rebel/McCray child would have pulled him out of his malaise? It would have helped him to see that life goes on even after tragedy."

"That boy is not a Rebel."

His mother was taking a stance and he had to do the same.

"I'm outta here."

Chapter Five

"Elias!" Before Elias could get out the door, Grandpa grabbed his arm. "No. I won't stand for this." Grandpa glanced at their mother. "You will not disinherit one of John's sons. I gave this land to my son just like my father gave it to me and his father gave it to him. Elias is a Rebel and this land is his heritage."

"Stay out of this, Abe," his mother said.

"I will not stay out of it. I'll invoke the codicil in John's will if I have to."

"What codicil?" Falcon asked. "I don't remember a codicil to Dad's will."

"Well, then you better read it again because there is one. It states that John Abraham Rebel shall retain ownership of his home and as many acres as he sees fit surrounding it until his death. Then it will become part of Rebel Ranch."

"So?" Falcon frowned. "That doesn't mean much."

"It means I can take five acres or a hundred acres or I can take it all back." Grandpa flung a hand at their mother. "I knew she'd try to pull something and I wanted to be able to protect my grandsons. I'll do anything to accomplish that."

Quincy got to his feet. "Grandpa…"

"Take it all back, Abe, if that's what you want to do."

His mother stormed out of the room and they heard her slam her bedroom door.

Elias had had enough. He put his arm around his grandfather's shoulders. "Grandpa, I'll be fine. I don't want you to do anything silly with the will. Leave it like it is. I'm a hard worker and I'll survive."

"No. I won't have it."

"Grandpa, let it go."

"Wait until things cool down," Falcon suggested to Elias.

"I'll talk to Mom," Quincy said. "Just stay on Rebel Ranch."

"Sorry, I can't do that." Elias walked out the door, and he could hear his grandfather screaming, "Elias!"

He quickly drove to his grandfather's house and grabbed a trash bag and dumped his clothes and shaving stuff inside. He then threw it into the back of his truck and headed out before Grandpa could make another scene. At the cattle guard he forced himself not to look back at everything he was leaving behind. Instead, he had to look forward to a future without Rebel Ranch. That was hard to swallow, but he had to make a decision based on what was best for his son.

Once he was out of sight of the house, he pulled over to the side of the road and grabbed his phone. He called Maribel.

"Is the kid asleep?"

"How did you get my number?"

"Is the kid asleep?" He wasn't in a mood to mince words.

"Yes. And I need to get some sleep, too."

"Call me when he wakes up."

"I will not."

He took a long breath. "The sheriff gave me full re-

sponsibility for Chase and I gave him my word. If you don't call me later this afternoon, I'll call Wyatt and he'll pick Chase up and put him back in jail. And I will not lift one finger to help him at the hearing. Do you understand me, Maribel?"

"You wouldn't do that."

"Try me."

"You're… You're…"

Elias cut her off by hanging up and drove on into town. He had to find a place to stay for the next few nights until he figured out what to do. Yesterday, his main worry had been getting hay off the field. Now he just needed a roof over his head. Life had dealt him a punch he hadn't been ready for.

The only place to get a room was at the new motel on the outskirts of town. Louann and her husband Charlie Polansky were the managers, and Louann was the biggest gossip in town. Gossip had never bothered him before, though, and he wasn't going to let it bother him now.

He went through the glass door and the bell over his head tinkled. Louann appeared from a side door behind the desk. She and Charlie lived on the premises. Her dyed blond hair was puffed up and layers of jewelry around her neck and on her wrists jingled as she walked.

"Elias Rebel, just the man I wanted to see. Your supposedly new son got our nephew in trouble. Brandon is a good kid and now look at the mess he's in. Thanks to you and your rambling ways. Who knew Maribel McCray had a son by you? Your mother must be livid."

Elias didn't even flinch. He leaned his forearms on the counter. "You like gossip, Louann? I got a good piece of gossip to share with Charlie. I bet he'd like to know where you were two Saturday nights ago, sitting in a booth down at Rowdy's with a man I'd never seen before."

Her blue eyes bulged out. "How…? How…?"

"The black wig didn't fool anybody, Louann. Now, I'd like a room."

"Room?" She recovered quickly. "Why do you need a room? There are all kinds of houses on the ranch."

Charlie walked in with a cup of coffee in his hand. "Hey, Elias. How's it going?" Charlie was a mild-mannered man with a pleasant personality and Elias liked him.

"I'm trying to get a room."

"I'll take care of it." He motioned for Louann to move aside. She frowned at him but stepped about three feet away, listening to every word.

"How long do you need it?" Charlie asked.

"I'm not sure. Maybe a week." Elias had no idea how long he would stay here. He could only take things day by day.

"We have a couple of suites you might like. They have a small kitchenette and a bigger bathroom."

"Does it have two beds?"

"Sure does."

"I'll take it." He reached for his wallet and pulled out his credit card. Charlie handed him the key and that was it. No questions asked. The way it should've been in the first place.

Charlie pulled a card from his pocket. "If you're interested in real estate, our daughter Gaynell is selling real estate these days."

Elias took the card. "Thanks, Charlie." He'd dated Gaynell back in high school a couple times and he didn't want to go down that road again. But he just might need a house.

He drove around to the room and went inside. He sat on the bed, pulled off his boots, jeans and shirt and then he crawled into the nearest bed. He'd been awake so long

his body was running on empty. But before sleep could claim him, two thoughts kept running through his head: he had a son. His mother had disinherited him.

FIVE HOURS LATER, Elias woke up, showered, shaved and changed clothes. There were several messages from his brothers on his phone, but he ignored them. He sat on the bed, trying to figure out his next move. Maribel and Chase needed a home and he had to find them one. He tried not to think about his mother. She was very stubborn and she had to come to grips with what had happened all those years ago. He had to give her time. In the meantime, he had to make a life of his own.

He saw Gaynell's card on the nightstand where he'd put it earlier. Although he hated to do business with an old girlfriend, he needed her help. He tapped in her number.

"Elias, I never thought I'd hear from you. You do know I'm married now."

He gritted his teeth. "I'm looking for a house in Horseshoe. Do you have anything to show me?"

"A house? Don't you live on the ranch?"

He sighed inwardly. "I want to buy a house, Gaynell. Do you want to sell me one? I'm not getting into a long conversation about where I live. I just want to make a deal."

"Okay, okay. Don't get in a snit."

"Do you have anything?"

"Yes. There are a few houses for sale."

"I'll meet you at the courthouse in an hour."

"What? This is Sunday, Elias, and I do have a family."

"Okay, I'll find another real estate agent because I'm buying a house."

"You're just as ornery as you ever were."

"So what's it going to be?"

"I'll meet you at the courthouse in an hour and a half. I have to take my daughter to a party first."

"I'll see you then." He laid his phone on the bed. He might be jumping the gun, but he hadn't paid child support in seventeen years so he felt he owed Maribel and Chase something. They needed a home and he could give them one.

Meeting Gaynell again was like picking up Jell-O with your fingers, messy and frustrating. She was a younger version of her mother with the dyed big blond hair and the jewelry. She'd gained about twenty pounds since high school and the tight pants and four-inch heels showed it all.

"Aren't you going to say how great I look?" she asked.

"Why would I do that?"

She slid her purse over her shoulder in an angry gesture. "You know, in high school I just wanted to smack you most of the time because you were so insensitive. Still are."

"Now, I don't think your husband would appreciate me giving you compliments, and I'd rather keep this on a business level."

"Yeah." She pulled out her laptop from her purse and laid it on the hood of his truck. "Here's what I have in Horseshoe." She flipped through several houses and he didn't like any of them.

"I was hoping for something bigger with a yard."

She flipped through some more.

"Wait. You just passed an Austin stone house."

"You don't want that one. It's run-down and needs a lot of work. It's been on the market eight years and each year it gets worse and the owners do nothing to keep it up."

"I want to look at it."

"Elias…"

"Let's go." He jumped into his truck and with a sigh

she got into her car and he followed her to the end of Mulberry Lane.

The house was just as she'd said—run-down. The grass was about three feet high and growing into the window screens. Trash littered the yard and it looked unkempt. Gaynell had a key and opened the front door. The stench almost knocked him backward. The roof leaked and the carpet was wet and mildewed. One of the bedrooms had a hole in the ceiling where it had rotted through and animals could go in and out. Overlooking the stench and the overall condition of the house, he could see it had once been a beautiful home. The kitchen, living room and dining room were open concept and featured a huge stone fireplace. There were three bedrooms, three baths, a study and a huge patio. The house sat on ten acres and there was a small barn out back. It would take some work but he felt he could turn this house into a home. He had the time.

"Who's the owner?"

Gaynell held her nose. "Can we talk outside? The smell is killing me."

They walked outside. "Todd Spencer and his sister own the house after their parents died. They live in Maryland and they haven't been here since the funeral. They're asking two hundred thousand, which is insane."

"Did you send photos?"

"No."

Elias went back into the house and took pictures of everything, even the barn with the tree caved in on the roof. Then he went back outside to Gaynell. "Call the owner. I want to talk to him."

"You can't be serious. This place is a mess."

"Call him."

"Are you going to make him an offer?"

"I might."

"You're as crazy as you always were."

"Call."

As soon as Gaynell had the owner on the phone, Elias took the phone from her. She tried to take it back, but he held on. "Mr. Spencer, Elias Rebel here. I would like to talk to you about your house in Horseshoe, Texas."

"Sure. We've been trying to sell it for a long time and we'd be happy to make a deal with you."

"Before I make you an offer, I want you to see the condition of the house. I'm going to send you photos of everything from my phone. It's in pretty bad shape. There's even a hole in the roof in one of the bedrooms and a tree fell on the barn. It's going to take a lot of work and money to fix it up. Once you look at the pictures, call me back."

Elias quickly attached all the photos and sent them to Mr. Spencer and then they waited. Fifteen minutes later, Mr. Spencer called.

"I had no idea the house was in such a mess."

"I'm going to make you an offer. You can take it or leave it. It's up to you, but I can have cash in your bank account as soon as you sign papers. Think about it." He told him the price and clicked off.

Gaynell laughed. "Are you serious? He's never going to take that amount. It's way too low. Besides, he received an offer about eight months ago of one hundred and fifty thousand, but it fell through because the buyer couldn't get the money."

"We'll see."

Gaynell glanced at her gold watch. "I don't really have the time to stand around waiting. I have to pick up my daughter in an hour."

"Let's give him fifteen minutes. In the meantime, I'm going to look around a little more." The house had a lot of

potential and he hoped the Spencers agreed to the deal, but he would look elsewhere if they didn't. Ten minutes later, he walked back to Gaynell.

She was sitting in her car, smoking a cigarette. He'd forgotten she had that filthy habit. "Still lighting up, huh?"

Getting out of the car, she threw the cigarette on the paved driveway and then she crushed it with the tip of her high heel. "I guess you're buying this house for Maribel."

He didn't respond because he felt it was none of her business.

"Who would've ever thought that you and Maribel got together back in high school? Since the Rebels and Mc-Crays didn't associate with each other, I wonder how that happened."

Luckily, his phone buzzed, preventing him from saying something he would have regretted. It was Mr. Spencer. He took the deal.

"Thank you, Mr. Spencer. Before I hand you over to the agent, I'd like your permission to start work on the house tomorrow."

"Sure thing. If the deal falls through, at least maybe the house will be cleaned up."

"It's not going to fall through." He handed the phone to a stunned Gaynell.

She talked for a few minutes, setting up the deal and then she clicked off. "I can't believe he took that deal."

"He wants it done as soon as possible. How long will it take?"

"We've already done the title search when we had the other offer so it shouldn't take long."

His cell buzzed again and he looked at it. It was Maribel with a text.

He's awake.

At least she had gotten the message that he wasn't going to cop out on his responsibility to Chase. "I've got to go. Call me when you have the papers ready to sign."

"You might need this." She tossed the keys to him.

"Thanks," he muttered, walking away.

"Give Maribel my regards!" she shouted after him.

He wasn't listening. He was bracing himself for another argument with Maribel.

Chapter Six

Maribel woke up at six in the afternoon. She hurriedly took a shower and changed clothes. She hadn't meant to sleep this long, but she had been exhausted from being up all last night. She'd gotten an hour or so of sleep in the morning and then she'd fixed lunch for Rosie and Jake. Their cousin Remi, who was married to Paxton Rebel, then came over with her daughter, Annie. That gave Maribel time to take a long nap.

Jake and Annie were playing in the living room and Rosie and Remi were sitting on the sofa, talking. "I have to check on Chase," she said over her shoulder as she walked toward Phoenix's office. Chase slept on the sofa in there, which occasionally caused a problem because Phoenix once in a while liked to do some work before going to the ranch. He and Paxton were going into the rodeo contracting business.

"He's up," Rosie said. "He just came into the kitchen for a glass of milk and a sandwich."

Chase pulled a T-shirt over his head as she walked in. "We need to talk."

"Ah, Mom. I've already said I'm sorry. Do we have to talk about it again?"

She folded the sheet and the blanket on the sofa and placed them neatly on the end. "Yes, we do." She took a

seat. "Before I start, I want you to remember that you're the one who caused all this trouble. And we can't go back and change anything."

Chase sat beside her. "So what happens?"

"Elias will be here soon and you have to go with him."

Chase jumped to his feet. "No. I'm not going with him."

She'd never forced Chase to do anything he didn't want to do, except maybe move to Horseshoe. But now she would have to pull out all her motherly instincts to get him to do the right thing. "If you don't, you'll have to go back to jail and Elias will not help us at the hearing. That means you're probably looking at jail time. So it's your choice. Elias knows a lot of people in this town and they respect him and we need him on our side to get out of this. Otherwise, it's looking very dim."

Chase stood there, defiance in every bone of his body. The older he got the more he looked like Elias. Chase had the same stubborn lines on his face, as if they were chiseled by the hand of the devil, which he'd inherited from his father. Elias certainly had a lot of devil in him. He had been the bad boy in school and girls were attracted to him. Sadly, she was no different.

"Where's he going to take me?"

"Probably to the ranch. There are a lot of people there you're related to and you might enjoy meeting them."

"No, I don't want to. I'm not a Rebel and I don't care about any of them."

With a mother's wisdom, she said, "Someday you will." She stood. "Pack your things and please be on your best behavior. I expect that from you. Okay?"

"Okay," he replied in a sullen tone. "But I don't have to like it."

As she went back into the living room, she heard a knock at the door. "It's probably Elias. I'll get it."

Elias stood there with the same brooding expression as Chase's. "Can I talk to you for a minute…in private?"

"Now what?" she asked as she stepped outside.

"I did something today I need to tell you about." He seemed nervous and that surprised Maribel. Very little upset Elias.

"What?"

"Well, the way I figure it, I owe you back child support."

She shook her head. "You don't owe me anything."

"Oh, but I do."

"Elias…"

"I bought a house for you and Chase."

"What! How dare you think that you can buy a house for me and Chase. I've taken care of him for seventeen years and I can continue to do so without your input."

"You're living in my brother's house and Chase is having a hard time adjusting. Rosie needs peace and quiet and I would think you'd be willing to give her that."

Oh, he was good. He was working her. "I'm not accepting a house from you."

"Sorry, I've already bought it and I'd like to show it to you."

She placed her hands on her hips. "You have some nerve."

He looked her straight in the eye. "And so do you. But before you get your feathers ruffled, I want to show you something." He pulled a piece of paper out of his shirt pocket and handed it to her. "I called Gabe. He's a lawyer. You should remember him."

"Yes." She remembered Gabe. He was Miss Kate's younger brother. When Miss Kate's mother had died, Gabe had lived with the Rebels until he'd graduated high school and went off to college.

"I asked him about child support. He said it's calculated

according to what I make. So we did some figures." He pointed to the paper in her hand. "The first number is the amount of child support I owe you. The second number is the amount I paid for the house. And the last number is what's left and I will use it to fix up the house. It's in bad shape, but I can make it like new. I have the time."

She frowned. "Isn't it hay season? And you work around the clock almost."

That nervous expression flirted with his face again and she knew something was wrong.

"I talked with my mother and it didn't go well."

"She doesn't believe Chase is your son, does she?" She had that feeling deep in her gut.

"No. She admits that you came to the house that day long ago and so does Grandpa, but…"

"She thinks I'm after you for money?"

"She's having a hard time with it and that's all I'm going to say."

There was so much more and she could see it in his eyes and she wasn't going to let it go. "Why won't you be working on the ranch?"

"Okay, Maribel, you want the truth, I'll tell you the truth." His words were sharp and edgy. "She said Chase wasn't my son and I told her he was. After going over that several times, she stood strong in her belief that Chase is not a Rebel. I told her I was out of there. And she said if I left she would disinherit me. I left."

Maribel was stunned. Elias had walked away from everything he'd worked for all his life because of his son… and her. She felt bad that he'd had to make that choice. She'd never wanted that to happen.

"I'm sorry, Elias." She meant every word and all the hard feelings she'd had against Elias were coming undone inside her like a ball of yarn. She looked down at the paper

in her hand. He'd gone through a lot of trouble to find a place for them in a short amount of time. And she needed a place to call home. Her pride was holding out, though. It was hard to accept his gift. But, as Miss Vennie had once told her, sometimes in life you have to deal with the hand you've been dealt.

"I know you mean well…"

"I rented a room down at the new motel for me and Chase and you can continue to live here and help Rosie while I'm working on the house. Two months, tops and I'll have it ready."

It sounded perfect but she was old enough to know that there was no such thing as perfect. She also knew better than to look a gift horse in the mouth. "Okay. I'll look at the house, but first I have to prepare Chase."

Ten minutes later, they were in Elias's truck and heading for Mulberry Lane. Maribel vaguely remembered the area. It had nicer homes with well-kept yards. Elias drove into the driveway of a white Austin stone. It was worse than she'd expected.

"This is a dump," Chase said from the back seat.

She was thinking the same thing with the weeds growing into the windowsills and the trash in the yard. The unkempt appearance had her thinking this house wasn't for them.

"I told you it needs work so wait until you look through the whole house before you make a decision. It smells like mildew inside and once I get all the old wet carpet out and the wet Sheetrock it will smell differently. It needs a new roof. It needs a lot of new things. Just keep that in mind." Elias was trying to sell her on the house before she'd even walked into it.

They got out and walked through the grass to the front

door. The stench had them taking a couple of steps backward.

"Ye gads." Chase held a hand over his mouth and nose. "This is awful. We can't live here."

"Open the windows," she told her son.

Chase tried, but the window wouldn't move. Elias went over and yanked it up with one hand. "Use some muscles, son."

"Don't call me *son*."

Maribel tensed and she knew this would probably set the tone for their relationship. They were always going to be at odds.

The huge fireplace caught her attention. The mantle was beautifully carved and gorgeous and she liked the open concept with the kitchen, the breakfast room and the living room.

"Look up," Elias said.

The ceiling was a pop-up dome with more beautiful woodwork. She'd never seen anything like it and it didn't seem to have any water damage. A beautiful chandelier hung from it.

"There's one in the master bedroom, too."

She walked through the house trying to see it as it would be when it was finished. It had a lot of potential. It was a split plan with the master bedroom on one end and the other two bedrooms on the other end. The master bath took her breath away. It was very large with his and her vanities. And the closets were enormous. She would never be able to fill them up. As the thought crossed her mind, she knew she wanted the house. It could be home for her and Chase. The yard was big. Everything about the house was big.

"Hey." Chase came running in. "There's a barn out back and a tree has fallen on it and caved it in. We can't live here, Mom. It's a mess."

"Close your eyes," she said to her son. "Try to see the house with the smell gone, new floors, a new roof, new paint, and the barn without a tree on it. Try to see it as it used to be and as it will be again."

"Ah, Mom, I can't do that."

"I can."

"Does that mean…?"

She turned to Elias who was watching them with a keen eye. "We'll take the house on one condition."

"What's that?" he asked with a lifted brow.

"That Chase and I help with the house."

"The kid is going to help for sure, but I don't know about you, Maribel. You're kind of puny." His eyes slid over her slim frame and that angered her.

"Puny! I can work just as hard as you can." She glared at him, daring him to refute it. He didn't.

"Deal, then?"

"Deal," she replied. "Now, could you please tell me where my car is?"

"It's been impounded over at Bubba Wiznowski's garage. I'll take you over there."

Once again they got into the truck, and drove to the garage. Maribel had known Bubba from school and had always liked him.

All six-foot-plus and three-hundred pounds of Bubba grabbed Maribel in a bear hug. "You're a sight for these tired old eyes." He pushed her back to look at her. "My, my, you're more beautiful than ever, Maribel."

"Aw, Bubba, you always say the nicest things."

"And mean every one of them."

"Yeah, yeah," Elias muttered. "He also believes in the tooth fairy."

"Hey, Elias." Bubba slapped him on the back. "I heard

the news." Bubba's gaze rested on Chase. "I guess this is the new addition to the Rebel family."

Chase bridled just as Maribel had expected him to.

"It's taking some getting used to," Maribel said to cover-up Chase's rudeness. "I'd like to get my car, please."

"Sure thing." Bubba went inside the old gas station that had been there for fifty years and came back with her keys.

"What do I owe you?"

Bubba waved a hand. "For you, nothing."

Elias cleared his throat. "Wyatt is not going to be happy with that." He pulled out his wallet and handed Bubba some money. "Take it." Bubba wouldn't so Elias stuffed it into his pocket.

Maribel's car was inside the eight-foot chain-link fence that surrounded the back of the station. Bubba opened the gate and she looked at Chase and said, "I'll see you in the morning at the courthouse. Please be patient and polite."

"I don't have any choice. I'm in Hicksville and I have to stay here. That sucks."

Maribel saw something she hadn't seen before. Chase needed a man in his life. He reacted to Elias because he knew Elias wasn't going to put up with his attitude, whereas she had always overlooked it. And she had put up with more than she should have. She turned and walked to her car.

"Wait, Mom. I need my football."

Football. Her son lived for the game.

After tossing him the ball, she got in her car and drove away. She hoped Elias treated his son just as his father had treated him—with a firm hand and a lot of love.

ELIAS DROVE TO the motel and Chase didn't say a word, which was a benefit. Elias needed a break to sort through

his thoughts. So much had happened in the last twenty-four hours and he was still reeling from the impact.

They walked into the room and Chase threw his duffle bag on the sofa and sank into a chair at the small table. "Well, this is better than that dump of a house."

Elias held his tongue and sat on the bed, facing his son. "We need to talk."

"About what?"

"Tomorrow morning and what's going to happen."

That cooled the boy's temper for a moment.

"You're in a very serious situation and I'll do my best to get you out it, but I need your cooperation. You need to show some respect to the judge, to the DA, to the sheriff and to me. Without that, you'll be sitting in a jail cell for a while. Do you understand?"

He nodded.

"Hiram Henley will be the judge and he's a stickler just like the sheriff. But he's also fair and known to give teenagers a second chance. He gave me one years ago and that might go against you. But then again, he knows me and how I've changed and if I tell him I'll keep you out of trouble, he'll believe me."

"What did you do?"

"You don't need to know that. You just need to know that I'll be in there fighting for you all the way. But you have to change your attitude and you need to change it now."

The football lay on the table and Chase picked it up. "All I want is to be able to play football and go to the NFL."

"That road starts with how things turn out tomorrow."

Chase twisted the ball in his hand. "My mom said that you left the ranch because of me."

He didn't want his son to be burdened with that fact and

he tried to soften it. "Let's just say my mom and I don't see eye-to-eye. But we'll work things out eventually."

"How do you know that?"

"Because I know my mother and I know that I've hurt her and it will take time for all of us to adjust to this new situation. But just know, you're my son and I will fight for you with my last breath."

The kid didn't say anything, just kept staring at the football. Elias wasn't sure what else to say. He'd pretty much said everything that was in his heart and that was something he never did. He was just feeling his way through all the emotions that seemed to be bubbling up inside him. He really needed to get some sleep. As he stood up, a knock sounded at the door.

"It's probably Mom," Chase said. "She's worried you're going to be mean to me."

If it was Maribel, he might just lose his cool. And if it was Louann, he really would lose it.

He yanked open the door and Grandpa stood there. For a moment, Elias was speechless. He looked outside to see if Quincy had brought him, but Grandpa's old Chevrolet truck was parked next to his.

"Grandpa, are you driving?"

"Of course, how do you think I got here?"

"You don't drive in the dark and you hardly drive at all. What are you doing here?"

Grandpa pushed past him into the room. "Stop asking so many questions. I came to meet my great-grandson."

"Grandpa—"

"Just cool your heels, okay?"

Elias gritted his teeth and he didn't know how much more he could deal with today. His nerves were on the brink of exploding and Grandpa had just lit the fuse.

Chapter Seven

"Who are you?" Chase asked as Grandpa walked up to him.

"I'm John Abraham Rebel, your great-grandfather."

"I don't know you." Chase didn't say it rudely. He was just stating a fact.

Grandpa slid into the chair across from Chase. "That's about to change." Staring at Chase, Grandpa shook his head. "My, my, that apple fell right under the tree."

"What are you talking about?" Chase asked.

"You look just like your father."

"Everybody says that. I don't see it."

"Well, then you need to buy a mirror, or even better…" Grandpa reached for his wallet in his back pocket. He pulled out several photos and laid them in front of Chase. "See if you can pick out Elias."

Chase pointed to one.

"Yep. That's him with his brother Egan. They were about thirteen and fourteen at the time. And look at that one. That's Elias at fifteen. Now tell me you don't look like him."

"I guess we favor."

"You sure do."

Grandpa and Chase kept talking and Elias stood there with one thought on his mind: Grandpa carried pictures of

him. He didn't know why that shocked him. Quincy was Grandpa's favorite. Normally that wouldn't have bothered him or affected him either way. But today, it seemed to pierce his heart in a good way.

"Do you like hamburgers?" Grandpa's words caught his attention.

"Yeah."

Grandpa looked at Elias. "Go down to the diner and get us some hamburgers. I haven't eaten supper and the boy is hungry."

Before Elias could respond his phone buzzed. He had a text from Quincy.

We can't find Grandpa. He was supposed to eat at our house tonight. Is he with you?

"Grandpa, Quincy is looking for you. You're supposed to eat at his house tonight."

Grandpa waved a hand at him. "Tell him I'm busy."

Elias took a deep breath, knowing Grandpa wasn't going to budge. That stubborn gene ran all the way through the Rebel family. He texted Quincy.

Grandpa's okay. He's here. I'll get him home ASAP.

He got a quick text back.

Where's here?

Elias didn't answer because he didn't want the whole family piling in on Chase. It would be too much.

"Are you getting hamburgers or what?" Grandpa asked. "And get a piece of pie, too. I want coconut." He looked at Chase. "What kind do you like?"

"Chocolate."

Grandpa thumbed toward Elias. "He likes chocolate, too."

Elias picked up his hat from the bed, knowing he was fighting a losing battle. He walked out the door leaving Chase in Grandpa's hands. When he came back, he could hear Chase laughing through the door. It was a magical sound. Up until now, he'd only heard anger in his voice.

He set the bag of food on the table and they dug in. Chase unwrapped his hamburger. "Grandpa was telling me about you when you were younger."

Grandpa.

Chase must have seen the shock on Elias's face. "He said for me to call him that."

"I sure did," Grandpa added. "That's who I am."

As they ate, Elias had to wonder if Chase would ever call him *Dad.*

After the meal, Grandpa went to the bathroom. When he came back, he went to the bed near the window and removed his shirt. He sat down and took off his boots and then his jeans. He crawled into bed.

What the...?

"Chase, find me the Western channel."

Chase got to his feet, eager to help. "I don't know where it is."

"Get the remote. You can find it."

Chase sat on the bed next to Grandpa and flipped through the channels.

"That's it!" Grandpa shouted. "That's Clint Eastwood. You know Clint Eastwood?"

"I know Scott Eastwood."

"Same thing. Elias, get me another pillow."

Groaning inwardly, Elias grabbed one out of the closet

and tossed it to Chase. He tucked it behind Grandpa's head. "Do you need another?" Chase asked.

"Nah. This is just right. Now let's see what ol' Clint is up to."

Elias drew a long breath and went into the bathroom just to get some quiet. Grandpa was making things worse. But on the other hand, he and Chase had made a connection and that was good. He just wanted to go to bed and forget this day had ever happened. There was no going back, though. Elias's free loving days were over. Responsibility felt like a yoke around his neck. He had to be the man his father had raised him to be. He had to be a father.

He sent Quincy a text.

Grandpa will be home tomorrow.

Feeling better he walked back into the room. Grandpa was snoring and the TV was blaring.

"He's asleep," Chase said.

"Yeah. That's why he likes the TV on. It helps him to go to sleep." He nodded toward the bathroom. "Time to go to bed."

Chase was back in a minute in his boxers and a T-shirt and slid into bed with Grandpa. Elias wanted to say something but for once words eluded him. They all needed to get some rest. He turned off the TV and the light and crawled into bed with a sigh of relief.

THE NEXT MORNING, Elias awoke at 5:00 a.m. and wanted coffee. There was none in the room, only a coffeemaker. He quickly showered, shaved and changed clothes and then got in his truck and went to the store to get breakfast tacos and coffee. Grandpa woke up when he smelled

the coffee. They had a quick breakfast and everyone got ready for the day.

As he walked outside, Elias said, "It's time for you to go home, Grandpa. Quincy's waiting for you."

"I'm not going home until I know this boy gets justice."

"I can take care of it."

"I know you can. I just want to give you some support. That's what grandfathers do."

Elias gave up. There was no arguing with his grandpa. They made it to the courthouse by 7:30 a.m. Maribel stood outside, waiting. He hardly recognized her in a black pantsuit and a white silk blouse. Her hair was up in a neat bun and she looked sophisticated and sexy. His mind went back to all those years ago and that dirt road.

"There's Mom," Chase said, and jumped out of the truck as Elias pulled into a parking spot.

Elias and Grandpa joined them. Grandpa shook Maribel's hand.

"I'm sorry I didn't do more all those years ago."

"It's okay, Mr. Abe. It happened the way it was supposed to happen, I guess."

"I'm going inside to talk to Hardy and Wyatt," Elias said. He went up the stairs toward the courtrooms and saw Hardy and Wyatt talking in the hallway. Elias joined them and they all shook hands.

"Don't try to influence us," Hardy said.

"Now why would I do that?" He looked at the DA and the sheriff. He'd known them all his life. Although at times he'd been on the other side of the law, they'd remained friends all these years. He felt he could say what he wanted to.

He looked at Hardy. "I just want to remind you that you know more about what I'm feeling since you found out you were a father when your daughter was ten years old.

It's not a good feeling and I know you'd do anything for Erin, just like I'm going to do everything I can for Chase."

"Elias, it's not the same thing."

"All I'm asking is for a fair shake for my kid. I'm in his life now and I'm going to make sure he does the right thing and makes good decisions."

"He broke the law," Wyatt said.

Elias stared at Wyatt. "What if it was Jody?" Jody was Wyatt's sixteen-year-old daughter.

"Jody is a straight-A student and she knows better."

"My son is a straight-A student, but the move from Dallas derailed him. He made a mistake and I'm asking you to give him a break. Just be fair, that's all I'm asking."

Maribel, Chase and Grandpa came up the stairs and Hardy and Wyatt walked into the courtroom.

"What did they say?" Maribel whispered to him as Grandpa and Chase made their way into the courtroom.

Maribel's eyes were worried. So were Elias's. "They're being tough, but I can be tough, too."

"Elias…"

They took their seats on the right in the courtroom. Chase sat between Maribel and Elias and Grandpa sat next to Maribel. The Wentz and Polansky families sat on the left. Wyatt and Hardy were at a table facing the judge. It was an informal hearing to decide if the crime warranted going to trial. Elias had declined an attorney, as had the Wentz and Polansky families. They were counting on the fairness of the judge.

Judge Henley walked in with his secretary and stenographer. Everyone stood until the judge took his seat at the bench. The judge was of medium height and balding and wore round wire-rimmed glasses. His secretary handed him a cup of coffee and he took a sip, then he glanced at the DA.

"What do we have, Hardy?"

Hardy stood and handed the judge a folder. "Three teenagers stealing beer around Horseshoe."

"Good heavens." The judge looked at Brandon and Billy Tom. "Don't your parents have beer at home?" Sometimes the judge tended to have a sense of humor and Elias was relying on it.

Mike Wentz got to his feet. "The new kid in town talked them into it."

The judge looked down at the folder. "Who's this new kid in town?"

"Chase McCray," Hardy replied.

"Is he one of the McCray family?"

Maribel got to her feet. "No, Your Honor. I'm Maribel McCray and Chase is my son. We moved away before he was born and we lived in Dallas. I recently returned home to help my sister Rosemary."

"It says here that Elias Rebel is his father?"

"Yes, Your Honor, he is."

The judge shook his head. "Lord help us all."

Elias got to his feet to say something, but the judge waved him down. "Wait your turn. I'm taking the other two boys first." The judge studied the folder.

Then he looked at Brandon and Billy Tom. "Two star football players making a mistake like this. What were you thinking?"

Mike got to his feet again. "Your Honor—"

"Sit down, Mike. I want to talk to the boys."

Billy Tom and Brandon stood. "It was stupid," Billy Tom said. "We made a mistake and we won't do anything like that again."

"I hope not."

The judge glanced at Hardy. "Any suggestions?"

"Billy Tom's and Brandon's records are clean and I'm

inclined to be lenient. Probation would be fine with the state."

"Sounds good to me. Billy Tom Wentz and Brandon Polansky, I sentence you both to one month of probation and once a week community service for a month. And you will pay for the stolen beer. You'll report to the sheriff. If you stay clean during that month, this will be expunged from your record. And you better win the state championship this year. You're free to go."

The family strolled out of the courtroom, but the boys looked back at Chase, who remained stoic, looking straight ahead.

The judge turned to Hardy once again. "I see Chase McCray ran from the sheriff. What's your opinion?"

Before Hardy could stand, Grandpa got to his feet and Elias was too far away to pull him back down. "I got something to say, Hiram."

"What are you doing in my courtroom, Abe?"

"Chase is my great-grandson and I want to make sure you do right by him."

"Abe—"

"I got two words for you, Hiram. Jimmy Jack." Saying that, Grandpa took a seat and everyone stared at him. Elias had no idea what *Jimmy Jack* meant, but by the flush on the judge's face, Elias was sure that he did.

The judge recovered quickly. "I'd like to talk to Chase." Chase stood. "Yes, sir."

"What possessed you to run from the sheriff?"

Elias put his hand on Chase's back and he could feel him trembling. "Tell him the truth," Elias whispered.

"I was scared. I knew my mom was going to be so mad and disappointed in me so I just bolted. I knew it was a mistake, but I couldn't seem to stop myself. I'm sorry I hurt so many people. I just…"

"What?"

Chase glanced at Elias. "You see, I was upset with my mom for moving to Horseshoe. I'm a good football player and I'm hoping to get a scholarship to play ball in college. My coach told me I was that good and I believed him. But moving here, I felt all my dreams were ruined and I'd never get a scholarship from a small school. I… I was trying to get my mom to change her mind, I guess. It was very immature of me, as someone told me." He glanced at Elias again.

"What position do you play?"

"Wide receiver."

The judge turned to the sheriff. "Is that true, Wyatt?"

"Yes, judge, I spoke to the coach this morning and he said Chase was a very good football player and he was sorry he wasn't going to be playing for the team this year. He said he's very talented and he will be missed by the school. The coach said he's never been in trouble and is always on time for practice."

Elias got to his feet and this time he wasn't sitting down. "Judge, I'd like to say something."

"Go ahead, Elias."

"I'm hoping you'll give my kid a second chance. He has a lot of me in him and I made a lot of mistakes as a teenager. You know that, but my dad kept me on track. I think I turned out to be a pretty good person, considering all the hijinks I got into with friends. If you release Chase into my custody, I will stick to him like grease on a pig. And I'll keep him on the straight and narrow."

"You spend too much time with your grandpa," the judge remarked.

"And that's a good thing," his grandpa shot back.

The judge turned to Wyatt and Hardy once again. "What do you suggest, Hardy?"

Wyatt was the one who answered, "I trust Elias on this one. I believe he can turn Chase around. That's just my opinion."

"I suggest two months' probation and one day a week for two months of community service," Hardy said. "If he stays clean, everything will be expunged from his record."

The judge banged his gavel. "Done. Everyone's free to go. Chase, you have to check in with the sheriff later."

"Yes, sir. Thank you."

Everyone got to their feet and Elias walked over and shook Hardy's and Wyatt's hands. "Thank you. I appreciate you giving my kid a second chance."

"I'm holding you to your word, Elias," Wyatt replied.

"You got it."

The judge stepped down from the bench and Elias shook his hand, too. "Thank you, Your Honor. I promise Chase will never be in trouble again or he will answer to me."

"Elias, I don't doubt it for a minute."

They filed out of the courtroom and the knot in Elias's chest eased. His son wasn't going to spend any time in jail. They walked out to Elias's truck and Maribel and Chase hugged.

Maribel stroked Chase's face. "I told you Elias would help us."

"Yeah," Chase murmured.

Maribel walked up to Elias. "Thank you."

There was something in her voice that bothered him. "You don't seem all that happy."

"I feel like I'm losing my son. I've raised him for seventeen years and the judge put him in your custody."

"Maribel, he'll be eighteen in November. Why don't we work on raising him together until then? I think we can manage that."

"I'm his mother and I will continue to make the decisions concerning his life. I want you to know that."

"I'm not in the mood to argue with you. Chase stays with me until his probation is over. We'll be working on the house and there won't be much time for anything else."

She glanced across the street to the diner. "I have an interview with Gladys in thirty minutes. I'm hoping to get the waitress job."

"We'll be at the house."

"Elias, please be patient with him. He doesn't know how to do anything except play football."

"By the time he reaches eighteen, he'll know how to do a lot of things. He'll know how to survive without his mother's help."

"Elias—"

"We're doing this my way."

She stomped her foot. "You're so… You're so…"

"Crazy."

"Yes, and bullheaded."

Unable to stop himself, he touched her nose with the tip of his finger. "And you love crazy."

Chapter Eight

Maribel walked across the street to the diner, infuriated with Elias. She was not crazy about him. She once was, but maturity had changed that and now she was just concerned about her son. For him, she would put up with Elias.

She took a minute to calm her nerves before going into the diner. It was the same as it had been when she was a teenager—the same table and chairs and the same pictures of bluebonnets on the walls. The linoleum was worn through in places and the dingy gray walls desperately needed a coat of paint. The faded dark blue booths had gray duct tape on some of them to cover tears.

The diner had probably been in Horseshoe a hundred years. Gladys' ancestors had owned it all that time. Gladys had to be in her eighties and Maribel didn't know how she kept up with the pace of running a diner. She and Gladys sat in the booth talking and within minutes she had the waitress job. It felt as if a weight had been lifted from her shoulders.

She drove to Rosie's to see how she was doing and changed clothes. Leah was there with her son, John, and Rachel, Egan's wife, was there with her son Justin. Everything was going fine. She told Rosie about the job.

Rosie clapped. "I'm so happy. Now you can stop worrying."

She sat beside her sister in the living room. "Now I'm worried about you. I won't be here all the time."

"Don't worry," Leah said. "Rachel, who won't go back to teaching until August, Remi and I have worked out a schedule so you can work. We're going to make sure this baby is born healthy."

"Thank you," Maribel said. She told them about the house and that she would be spending a lot of time there, too.

"That's wonderful," Rosie said. "You'll have your own home."

"Yeah, but I'll have to put up with Elias." She made a face and everyone laughed.

Thirty minutes later, she was at the house. Chase was standing outside with a mask over his nose and mouth.

"What's going on?"

"He's fumigated the house for roaches and ants and it stinks. Tomorrow, he says we're tearing out all the old carpet and linoleum. He's working on the roof now. I can't keep up with him."

She patted his chest. "You'll do."

Chase pulled off the mask. "We went to the city to have the water and the lights turned on and they said they couldn't get to it until the end of the week. He said, 'No way. I want it done now.' They turned it on. Then we went to the sheriff's office and I start my community service next Monday from eight o'clock to twelve o'clock. He paid for the stolen beer. All of it. He told the sheriff to tell Billy Tom's and Brandon's parents that he had taken care of it and I would work for every penny of it. Then we went to the hardware store and the lumberyard and then to Bubba's. He said he wanted to buy a flatbed trailer and Bubba said just take one. He said no, he wanted to buy one and they went round and

round. He wrote a check and laid it on Bubba's desk. I don't think Bubba's gonna cash it."

She noticed he wasn't calling Elias by his name. He was just saying *he*. Chase probably never would call Elias *Dad* but she was hoping he would at least call him *Elias*. It would take time.

"You've had a busy morning."

"Yeah. He knows how to get stuff done."

"You seemed to like Mr. Abe."

"Yeah. He's cool. He had to go home to feed his dog, but he said he would be back to help. So far he hasn't returned. I hope he's okay."

"I'm sure he is. Where's Elias?"

"He's on the roof tearing off the spot that has the hole. I have to go help him." Chase pulled on a pair of gloves. They walked around to the back of the house and they both went up the ladder to the roof. Elias was tearing off shingles like a crazy man. He had the trailer backed up to the house and was throwing them onto it.

Elias sat back on his heels. "About time you showed up. Start pulling some of the shingles off and throw them onto the trailer."

"With my hands?" Chase asked.

"Unless you can do it with your feet."

"No. I'll use my hands."

"The shingles are brittle and come off easily. There's no need for you to be up here, Maribel."

"I'll help Chase with the shingles, and please don't tell me what to do."

Elias wiped sweat from his brow. "Pigheaded as always. You'll need gloves."

"My hands will do fine."

"Suit yourself."

They worked until eight o'clock and by then they had all

the shingles off the roof. Elias worked on fixing the hole. Taking a breather, Maribel watched him. The muscles in his shoulders and arms rippled as he sawed away the rotted wood. His movements were precise and even. He was strong, confident and all male. That's what had attracted her to him in first place.

They'd put in a long day and they were all tired. A lot of progress had been made, though, because Elias never stopped working. Her son was learning a good lesson. Chase was wilted like a flower without any water, but he would survive.

Once they were on the ground, Elias asked, "Did you get the job?"

"Yes." She was happy to tell him. "I start tomorrow at six o'clock and work until two o'clock. I have the breakfast and lunch run. I'll be here just as soon as I get off."

Elias stored away his tools in the toolbox on his truck. "What about Rosie?"

"Leah, Rachel and Remi have it handled."

Elias pulled off his gloves and placed them on the dash. "I'm ready for a shower and some food." He looked at Chase. "How about you?"

"Yes, sir."

Chase was dirty from his head to his toes. She'd never seen him this filthy, even his tennis shoes were dirty. He wasn't complaining. That's what surprised her. She gave him a brief hug and said, "I'll see you tomorrow."

Walking away wasn't easy. She'd spent every day of her life with Chase and it was hard to be away from him, but she had to let go. Soon, he would be off to college. He would grow into a man and she had to learn to deal with that.

And with Elias's input.

ELIAS'S MUSCLES WERE tight and he needed a shower and some food. But he was pleased with the work they'd gotten done today. The boy hadn't complained once. That had shocked him, but they were working toward a common goal: a home for them.

As they drove in to the motel, Grandpa pulled in right beside them. Grandpa was starting to get on his nerves, but he knew the old man just wanted to help so he had to lighten up.

"It's Grandpa," Chase said and got out of the truck.

Elias watched as Chase hugged Grandpa. "I thought you were going to help us today?"

"Ah, I got caught up at the ranch, but I brought food. It's on the passenger side. Take it in and we'll have supper."

Chase looked at Elias, "Can I take a shower first?"

"I'd prefer it." Elias handed Chase the key and he went inside with the bag of food.

"What's going on at the ranch?" Elias asked Grandpa.

"Ah, your mother is holed up in the house and didn't take lunch to the guys today. Quincy called and said Jenny was fixing sandwiches and stuff and asked me to pick it up and bring it out to the hay fields."

"Did someone check on her?" He didn't like the sound of this. His mother always brought food when they were working.

"Quincy did and said that she needed some time. She's just stubborn, that's all. She can't admit she made a mistake."

"Grandpa, you need to talk to Mom and tell her you're not doing anything about the will. I want you to do that." Elias thought that might bring his mother some peace.

"No way. Not until she admits she made a mistake and that she's not disinheriting you. I'm not bending this time. She has to."

"Grandpa…"

Grandpa walked into the room, completely ignoring him. He hated that his mother was hurting, and he was hurting, too. There had to be some resolution to all this. Right now, though, he was tired and needed rest.

Chase was in clean shorts and a T-shirt, digging food out of the bag.

"I'm taking a quick shower," Elias said.

When he came out, the food was on the table. Chicken fried steak and all the trimmings, and Grandpa had even bought kolaches from the bakery. Chase talked on and on, telling Grandpa what they'd done today. Elias never realized he talked so much. He kept saying *he* did this and *he* did that. It took a moment for him to realize that was what Chase was calling him. *He*. Like he couldn't say *Elias* or even, heaven forbid, *Dad*.

Afterward, Chase carried the trash out to the dumpster. Grandpa removed his clothes and crawled into bed, getting comfy. There was no need to tell him to go home because Elias knew he wouldn't.

Elias slipped out of his jeans and slid into bed with a sigh. Chase came back and he and Grandpa turned on the TV. Chase flipped around until he found the Western channel.

"John Wayne, that's a good one, boy. Leave it there."

Elias counted in his head because he knew it would be about fifteen minutes until Grandpa fell asleep. And he was right. He heard the snoring. To his surprise, Chase was asleep, too. He got up and turned off the TV and the light. Then he welcomed the darkness that claimed him. Tomorrow was another work day.

It just wouldn't be on Rebel Ranch.

ELIAS AWOKE AT five o'clock to make coffee. Then he went down to the convenience store and bought breakfast tacos. When he came back, Grandpa and Chase were up.

Just as they were getting ready to leave, there was a knock at the door. Elias opened it to find a very pregnant Paige, Jude's wife, at the door. The baby was due in July.

"Good morning, Elias."

"Paige, how did you find me?"

"I asked Grandpa."

She dug into her purse and pulled out a set of keys. Handing them to him she said, "These are keys to my mother's house, which is vacant. It belongs to me, my brother and my sister and you're welcome to use it."

He hadn't expected this and for a moment he was speechless. "Does my mother know about this?"

She lifted an eyebrow. "It may surprise you to know that I don't have to clear things with Miss Kate. It is my house and I can do what I want with it."

He thought about it for a minute and decided not to be stubborn or let his pride get in the way. They needed more space.

"It has three bedrooms and two baths and it's furnished sparingly, but there is a washer and a dryer. Water and electricity are on. Please use it. Now I have to get to work."

Paige was an OB/GYN doctor. She was the love of Jude's life. They'd gotten pregnant in high school and had decided to give the baby up for adoption because Paige had a full scholarship to med school. But Jude couldn't live with that decision and had raised their son alone. Twelve years later, Paige had come back and discovered that Jude had their son. There had been some ups and downs but eventually they'd gotten back together, and now they were expecting their second child.

"Thank you, Paige. I appreciate it."

"Use the house," she said as she hurried to her SUV.

"Who was that?" Chase asked.

"That's your Aunt Paige," Grandpa answered. "She's your Uncle Jude's wife. They have a son named Zane and he'll be a senior next year. In your class."

"I don't care. I don't want to meet him." Some of the old resentment surfaced in Chase's voice and Elias let it slide. It had to be hard to be thrown into a family he'd never met.

Grandpa patted Chase's shoulder. "Someday you will. Zane is a good kid and he'll show you around the school. But no one's pushing you."

Elias held up the keys. "Pack your things, kid. We're moving out."

Grandpa went home to feed his dog and to check and see if the brothers needed anything. Elias checked out of the motel and he and Chase drove over to Paige's house. It was three blocks away from Mulberry Lane, which was going to make it very easy to go to work.

"This is so cool," Chase said, walking through the house. "It's neat and clean and not like that motel room. It has space."

Elias thought it was cool, too. There was an old Formica table and chairs in the kitchen and a sofa, a chair and a small TV in the living room. Each bedroom had a bed and sheets and there was a dresser in the master bedroom.

"Can I call Mom and tell her?"

Elias handed him his phone. He talked for a minute and handed the phone back. Chase fidgeted and then asked, "Can Mom stay here with us?"

Elias had to think about living with Maribel and how it would affect him and her. They really were strangers. But he didn't want to upset Chase. "If she wants to."

On the way to Mulberry Lane, Chase asked, "Can I have my phone back?"

"Your phone is at the sheriff's office and you're not getting it back until you show some maturity and responsibility."

"But I can't talk to my friends in Dallas."

"That's what happens when you break the law. Been there, done that, kid. My dad took my truck away for a whole month one time and I thought I was going to die. Learned a big lesson. Never be stupid again."

"What did you do?"

"Bubba and I got drunk one night when we were about seventeen and decided to paint the Catholic church bell red. The Horseshoe community was not amused and it took me and Bubba about two days to scrub that red spray paint off that bell."

"You had a truck when you were seventeen?" That's all that Chase had picked up from his tell-all.

"I got a used truck when I was sixteen."

"Wow! My mom can't afford to buy me a truck, but she lets me drive her car."

"And we all know how that turned out." Elias hadn't meant to be so critical. It had just slipped out.

"You're never going to forget that, are you?"

"Probably not."

They went to work, tearing old tar paper off the roof and checking for rotted boards. By noon, they had all the new tar paper on. They picked up the scraps from the ground and loaded down the trailer to run to the dump ground. On the way back, they stopped at the Dairy Queen and got a hamburger. Chase had stayed right with him all the way. Even when Elias had pushed him, he hadn't balked. He had to admire the boy for that.

Next, they started tearing out the old carpet to get the smell out of the house. Elias was cutting it into strips to pull it out when Maribel showed up. She was absolutely

glowing, her eyes sparkled and a smile lit up her face. For a moment, Elias had a hard time catching his breath.

How was he going to deal with her on a daily basis?

Chapter Nine

"How did it go, Mom?" Chase asked.

"Great." Maribel was bursting with excitement. For once, everything was going right in her life and she felt happy. "Everyone was so friendly and nice and I learned the ropes easily. A lot of people came in who I knew as a teenager. I made thirty-two dollars in tips. Can you imagine? In Horseshoe, Texas?"

"Did you wear a low-cut blouse?" Elias asked.

He was on his knees cutting carpet and she kicked the back of his boot. "No, I did not. And if you say that one more time, I'll kick you higher."

He turned and sat on his butt. "Ah, Maribel, now there's the temper I remember."

She thought it best to just ignore him. "So what are we doing?"

"Getting rid of the old carpet." Chase pointed to the floor. "He's cutting it into big pieces and then he's going to stick it in the window and pull it onto the trailer, which he has parked right up to the window. I'm supposed to help."

"Let's do it, kid." It was hard work and it was getting late by the time they finished. Maribel was soaked with sweat. It had to be ninety degrees.

She had to talk to Elias and she wasn't looking forward to it. Elias let Chase drive the truck and trailer around to

the back of the house. That left them alone in the kitchen. The perfect time. "Chase told me about Paige's house."

Elias guzzled down a bottle of cold water. He wiped his mouth with the back of his hand. "Yeah, it's much better than the motel room."

She took a deep breath. "I brought my stuff from Rosie's and if you give me the key I'll go over and start supper."

"You will, huh?" His white T-shirt was brown and his jeans were caked with dirt. And yet, he still managed to look handsome with his dark hair falling across his forehead. She had to stand her ground and not let him get to her.

"I'm staying with my son," she stated.

"You do know that I will be living there, too."

"I'll just have to take the bad with the good."

He leaned in close to her face. "And the bad is very, very bad."

She stared him straight in the eye. "I can handle it."

He leaned against the cabinet and folded his arms. "Are you sure? What do you think the people in Horseshoe are going to say when they find out we're living together?" The devilish glint in his eyes made her that much more determined.

"Gossip doesn't bother me anymore." She lifted an eyebrow. "Unless it bothers you."

He laughed, a kind of a mocking sound. "I think you know the answer to that."

She held out her hand. "Keys, please. I'm not playing a cat-and-mouse game with you."

He stared at her for a moment and she resisted the urge to look away. Could he read her thoughts?

"Do you ever think about that night?"

"Keys, Elias." She wasn't having that conversation. Not today.

"They're on the dash of my truck."

"Thank you. I'll see you at the house."

"We're taking a load to the dump ground first."

She nodded and went out the back door to Elias's truck. Chase was sitting in the driver's seat.

"This is a cool truck, Mom. He's going to let me back up the trailer to the house tomorrow."

Chase was learning so much from Elias and she couldn't fault him for that. But she was just afraid her emotions were getting involved and she didn't want them to. She didn't want to be attracted to him again. She couldn't be.

"That's nice. Hand me the keys from the dash."

"You're going to the house?"

"Yes. I talked to Elias and I'm moving in."

"Cool."

It was anything but *cool*. It was survival, and she would do anything to stay with her son. Even banter with Elias.

She drove to the house and looked around. She then unpacked her things in the master bedroom. Yes, she was taking the master bedroom. Elias might have another opinion, but she wasn't budging.

Taking a quick shower, she decided to wash her hair because it was filthy with dust. Then she put on shorts and a tank top and headed for the grocery store. She bought extra things like milk and cereal and chocolate chip cookies because Chase loved them. She didn't stay too long, though, as she had to cook supper.

As she finished making a salad, the guys came in. "I'm taking a shower," Chase called as he headed down the hall.

"Me, too," Elias said and went toward the master bedroom.

She was putting the steaks on plates when Elias walked in. "It's almost ready," she told him.

"You put your things in the master bedroom."

"Yes." She turned to look at him innocently. "Is that a problem?"

"Could be. You should've asked."

She fluttered her eyelashes and felt like an idiot. "May I please have the master bedroom?"

He pulled out a chair and sat down. "That doesn't work on me."

She wasn't sure what worked on Elias, but she wasn't moving out of the master bedroom.

They sat down to eat and Chase did all the talking about what they did and what they were going to do. And he continued to call Elias *he*. There was admiration in his voice, though, but he never once referred to Elias by name or anything else.

She and Chase were putting dishes in the dishwasher when there was a knock at the door.

"I bet it's Grandpa." Chase ran to the door and came back with Grandpa in tow.

Elias stood up to confront his grandpa. "Why are you driving at night?"

"I can drive anywhere I want."

Elias sighed. "Have you had supper?"

"Yeah. I had to eat at Quincy's to pacify him." Grandpa looked around. "Is there a TV in here?"

"There's a small one in the living room," Chase said and looked at Elias. "Can I put it in my bedroom?"

"Sure. I think it gets one channel."

Chase and Grandpa worked with the TV and she was left alone again with Elias.

He sat down at the table. "That old man is going to drive me crazy."

Maribel finished wiping the cabinet and took a seat across from Elias. "He just misses you."

"I guess. He falls asleep in his chair and I wake him

up every night and tell him to go to bed. Who knew that was so important?"

"Sometimes it's the little things that count."

Elias took a drink of his iced tea and there was silence for a moment.

"It was nice of Paige to offer the house. I'll make sure everything is cleaned and washed when we leave."

"I'm sure she'd appreciate that." He got to his feet. "I better check on Grandpa."

In a minute, he was back. "They're both asleep with *Cowboys and Aliens* playing on the TV. I don't think that's Grandpa's type of Western."

He sat down again and took a swallow of tea. "I have a lot of questions, Maribel."

Her nerves tinged with dread. "Well, I don't feel like answering them."

"Did you not think once in all these years to pick up the phone and call me and tell me about Chase?" He wanted answers and she had a feeling he knew how to get them.

"No," she answered honestly. "I would never have called Rebel Ranch after what your mother had said. I wasn't that brave back then. Chase and I found a home and life was good."

"I had a right to know."

"Why do we have to rehash all this? It's done and I can't go back and change anything."

He twisted his glass. "Were you happy about the pregnancy?"

Maribel stared down at her hands clasped in her lap. "At first, no, but when my dad was beating me the first thing I did was cover my stomach. At that moment, I knew I wanted the baby and I would protect it with my life."

A frown etched across Elias's face. "Did your mother know you were pregnant?"

"Yes."

"And she didn't help you?"

This was the hard part, telling someone else about her mother. "No. All my life, my mother has said, 'I love you, Maribel,' over and over, but when it counted she did nothing. As a mother, I don't understand that. I stopped believing in love that day."

"You don't mean that. You love Chase and you love Rosie."

"They know I love them, but I'll never say the words to them. They don't mean anything. Actions speak louder than words."

"You need help, Maribel. I mean you need to talk to a therapist or something."

She stood. "Shut up, Elias." She turned and walked into the master bedroom. Inside she was trembling and it took a moment for her to calm down. No one understood how she felt. That pain went deep and she didn't want to feel it again. Ever.

She stripped out of her clothes and pulled a big T-shirt over her head. As she reached to pull back the covers, Elias walked in dressed in jockey shorts and a T-shirt.

"What…"

"The other bedroom has a three-quarter bed and it's too small for me. I won't get any rest and I need my rest. I'm sleeping in here. It has a king-size bed."

"You are not sleeping in here. You'll just have to make do."

He smiled a crooked smile and she knew she'd lost. "I don't think so." He crawled into the bed as bold as ever.

"Elias…"

He reached up and turned off the lamp and rolled onto his side. "Good night, Maribel. You can sleep in here or in the other room. Your choice."

"You're... You're...so..."

"Crazy?"

"And infuriating." She stomped out of the room and went across the hall to the other bedroom. He had her so wound up she wasn't going to sleep. And like him, she needed her rest. She counted to ten and calmed down.

What would he do if she slid into bed with him? That was the problem. Knowing Elias, she wasn't willing to chance it. But oh, would she love to get even.

ELIAS WOKE UP to the smell of bacon frying, which had his mouth watering. Hot damn! Maribel knew the way to a man's heart. And other places. She hadn't taken him up on his dare last night. He'd hated to uproot her from her little nest but he had needed sleep. He shaved, changed clothes and headed for the kitchen.

She was at the stove in tight jeans and a white knit top. Her hair was up in its customary ponytail.

"That's what I like, Maribel. A woman who can cook."

"Don't talk to me, Elias, or I just might smack you."

"Come on." He leaned against the counter, sipping coffee and watching her every movement. If she could have read his mind, she probably would have smacked him. There was no one as attractive as Maribel. "I couldn't sleep on that little bed"

"If that's an apology, I'll accept it. I'll move my stuff into the other room."

"You can still have the bathroom. I just want the bed."

"Whatever." She placed a platter of scrambled eggs and bacon on the table. "Chase, Mr. Abe, breakfast!" she called.

Chase ran in fully dressed and ready for the day. Grandpa trudged behind him. "Wow, Mom. This smells good. We usually have breakfast tacos."

"Sit down and eat. I have to go to work."

"Always liked a woman who could cook," Mr. Abe said.

She patted him on the shoulder. "It must run in the Rebel family."

She didn't wait for a response. She hurried to the bedroom to get her purse and phone and then headed for the back door.

"Chase, please put the dishes in the dishwasher before you leave so they'll be clean for tonight."

"Okay."

"You sure are bossy," Elias remarked.

"I haven't even started," she said. "All beds better be made when I come home."

Grandpa laughed and she loved that perplexed look on Elias's face.

Fifteen minutes later, Elias and Chase were out the door and headed for the house. Grandpa went home to do what he could at the ranch. They worked in one of the bathrooms, breaking up the old tile and pulling it out. At eight o'clock, they were at the lumberyard to pick up shingles. Elias had the trailer loaded down and they spent the rest of the day putting on a new roof. Teaching Chase was a test of his patience. He could have just done it himself but he wanted him to learn.

"I'm so slow," Chase complained.

"You'll get faster at it. Put the roofing nails in your hand and use your fingers to reach for the tip. You'll get the feel of it. Hold it down and hammer it in. Over and over. And try not to nail your fingers."

The kid was getting better.

"Hey, Elias." Jericho came up the ladder to see what they were doing.

Elias sat back on his heels. "What are you doing here? I'm sure they need you at the ranch."

"Falcon sent me into town to get more string and supplies. It's lunchtime so I thought I'd stop by and check on you. We sure miss you at the ranch. Falcon hired two teenagers and we're still behind. No one can do the work that you do."

Rico was a friend of his brother Egan. They met in prison when Egan had been unjustly accused of a crime he hadn't committed. Rico had saved Egan's life and for that their mother had offered him a job. No one regretted that decision. Jericho was a hard worker and loyal to the family.

Chase was staring at Rico and Elias realized he hadn't introduced his son. Rico was intimidating sometimes. He was well over six feet with long hair tied into a ponytail at his nape and a long slash marred his face. He was the type of dude you'd want to have your back every day of the week.

"Rico, this is my son, Chase."

Rico looked at Chase, closely.

"Go ahead and say it," Chase said. "Everyone else does."

"You look just like your dad."

"Yeah."

Elias waited for Chase to say something else, but he didn't. He was probably tired of hearing it, but then he was going to hear it for the rest of his life.

"Grab Chase's nail bag and let's show him how to put on a roof."

Chase stood back and watched as Elias and Rico nailed shingles to the roof as fast as they could.

"Wow!" Chase shouted. "I wish I had my phone so I could videotape this and put it on YouTube."

"And then we'd have to hurt you," Elias said jokingly.

Chase grinned, and for the first time, Elias felt a connection to his son.

WHILE CHASE HAD his first community service day, Elias drove to Temple to finalize the sale of the house. It didn't take long for him to sign the papers and send the money to the Spencers. It was a done deal. Gaynell raised an eyebrow when he had the deed put in Maribel's and Chase's names. It would be their home and he couldn't be happier. But his funds were dwindling and soon he would have to look for work.

On his way back to Mulberry Lane, he saw the Kuntz boys, Freddie and Scooter, and their cousin Leonard walking through a residential area. As boys known for stealing, that couldn't be good. He pulled over to the curb and rolled down his window. A lot of nights, Freddie and the boys hung around outside Rowdy's asking for beer. Elias never gave them any. No one in Horseshoe seemed to care about the boys, especially their mother. He hoped CPS could get them out of a bad situation.

"You got any beer, Elias?" Freddie asked.

"You know I'm not giving you beer. Where y'all going?"

Freddie came to the window and Scooter and Leonard hung back. "We're in summer school cause our grades are bad. The principal sent us home because we broke a computer. They're always picking on us."

"Hop in. I'll give you a ride home."

Freddie jumped in the passenger seat and the other two boys got in the back seat. Scooter was big and pudgy while the other two boys were skinny. Scooter had a learning disability and he didn't talk much. He just mumbled. He was in special ed classes and the kids made fun of him.

"Thanks, Elias. You're a good person."

"Just stay out of trouble, Freddie, and stay in school. Things will get better."

"Thanks, man."

Elias drove to the Dairy Queen and bought them hamburgers and drinks. He had a feeling there wasn't much food at home. It was a little thing, but they needed to know that someone in this town cared. There wasn't a father in their lives and the boys desperately needed guidance.

He thought about Chase growing up without a father, but Chase would have a father in his life from now on.

Chapter Ten

Every day they continued to work on the house. The roof was done and now they were concentrating on the inside. Chase finished his first community service day and came home all excited and eager to tell Maribel about everything.

"Billy Tom, Brandon and I worked on the community center. We had to sweep, mop and clean up. The sheriff said a high wind blew off some shingles and for us to nail them back on." The kid thumbed into his chest. "I told him I could do it and I showed Billy Tom and Brandon what to do and we had the shingles on in no time."

Her kid was proud of himself.

"Wyatt has all of you working together?" Maribel asked.

"Yeah. I didn't know how that was going to go. I didn't think we'd ever be friends again. I said I was sorry and that seemed to do the trick. And since *he* paid for all the beer we stole and their parents weren't out any money, that helped, too."

"Son, his name is Elias."

"I know." He looked down at his sneakers. "I don't know what to call him."

"You'll figure it out."

"Yeah. Anyway, we talked about football a lot. Billy Tom is the quarterback and Brandon's an offensive line-

man." He thumbed into his chest again. "And I'm the wide receiver who Billy Tom's going to throw to. Pee Wee is Brandon's younger brother and he's the running back. I met him today, too. We're going to win the state championship this year. For Judge Henley."

It was refreshing to listen to her son. Gone was the sourpuss of a week ago. He was putting down roots and making friends and finding out what small town life was all about.

Maribel had swept and mopped the whole house, but there was one piece of linoleum she couldn't get up in the kitchen. When Elias walked in, she was pulling with all her strength and her face was red from her efforts.

"Hold on." He went outside and came back with his ice chest and poured the cold water on the linoleum.

"What are you doing? Now I'll have to mop that up."

"Just wait a minute and you'll see what it will do, or at least what I hope it will do."

She sat back on her heels. "What is it supposed to do besides make a mess?"

"It's about ninety-five degrees today so the linoleum is very warm. The icy water will make it contract."

"It's making a popping sound."

"Try pulling it up now."

She stood up and, with her gloved hands, reached for the end of the linoleum and yanked. Not expecting it to be easy, she put more strength into it than necessary and went flying backward on the concrete. She just lay there completely still. Stunned and sore.

Elias fell down by her side. "Are you okay?"

"My pride is damaged. Or is that my butt?" She turned her head to glare at him. "Why didn't you tell me it would be easy to come off?"

"I thought I did."

"Yeah." She laughed. It was the first time she'd heard herself laugh since she'd made the decision to move back to Horseshoe. The sound vibrated through her whole body and her heart raced as she stared into Elias's dark eyes.

"You know, you have freckles right across the bridge of your nose."

"I'm well aware of that, Elias."

"I wonder what it would feel like to kiss them."

"Don't you dare."

"Ah, Maribel, don't you know better than to say things like that to me."

"Eli…" Her breath caught in her throat as he gently kissed the bridge of her nose. She couldn't breathe. She couldn't move. All she could do was enjoy the sensation that made her want to laugh again from the sheer pleasure of it. She sat up to stop the crazy thoughts in her head. She couldn't let anything happen between her and Elias. It had taken too long to get over him the first time.

"I better go home and start supper." She slowly got to her feet.

"Go home and soak in a hot tub. The kid and I will pick up Mexican food."

"That's nice, Elias." She tapped his dirty T-shirt with one long finger. "You better be careful or everyone will think you're getting soft."

"Not anyone who knows me."

MARIBEL WENT HOME and soaked in a hot bath. She heard the guys come in and leave again. She dressed in shorts and a tank top and went to the kitchen to make iced tea. The guys came back with bags of Mexican food and Mr. Abe was with them.

They sat at the kitchen table talking and eating. Or rather, Chase and Mr. Abe were doing all the talking. Ma-

ribel was tired, more so than usual. She got to her feet
"I'm going to soak in the tub again. Good night, everyone."

"Good night," echoed behind her.

She filled the tub with warm water and sprinkled lavender salts in it. It was soothing and relaxing and she let the warm water ease all the aches and pains from falling backward on the concrete floor. Her thoughts drifted to the house.

She'd had her doubts when she'd first looked at it, but now she was excited. Elias was turning it into a really nice home for them. *Them.* What did that mean? Did that include Elias? She'd only been in Horseshoe a few weeks and Elias seemed like a part of her life now. Every day, she fought her attraction to him. But then he was Chase's father and she couldn't ignore that. Little by little, Elias was weaving his way back into her heart, and the emotions of that seventeen-year-old girl were still alive and well inside her.

But as the saying goes: you can never go back.

It shocked Maribel that she wanted to.

AFTER CHECKING ON Chase and Grandpa, Elias went to the master bedroom and slid into bed. Flipping off the light, he wondered how long Maribel was going to stay in the bathroom. His phone buzzed and he reached for it on the nightstand. It was Quincy with a text.

Come home. Talk to Mom.

He got the same message every day from his brothers, but Quincy was the most persistent. He was the peacemaker in the family and it was probably driving him crazy that he couldn't fix this without someone being hurt.

Elias missed the ranch and the work. He missed his

brothers and his mother. But he was content working on the house and being with his son. And with Maribel. He still had those same feelings for her as he'd had when he'd been a teenager. He'd always wondered how something that had felt so right could be so wrong. But to him it had never been wrong.

He flipped over and grabbed his phone again to look at the time. Maribel had been in the bathroom over an hour. What was she doing? Maybe something had happened. He jumped out of bed and knocked gently on the door.

"Maribel."

No response.

He tried again and still no response.

He tried the handle and the door wasn't locked. Stepping inside, he saw her in the bathtub, asleep. He wasn't a voyeur, but he stared at her for a full minute. The water did little to disguise her perfect feminine frame from her full breasts to her rounded hips and long legs. Oh, man. You don't stare at a naked woman like a teenager even when you care about her. There it was. He cared about Maribel. He'd cared about her for a long time. He grabbed a big towel and gently shook her. "Maribel."

She sat up straight, her eyes wild. "What…what…are you doing in here?"

"You've been in here over an hour and I came to check on you."

She tried to cover her breasts with her hands and the triangle between her legs.

With a sigh, he shoved the towel into her hands. "It's a little late for modesty."

"You had no right…" Her voice wandered off, as she was still half-asleep.

He reached for her T-shirt on the vanity and slipped it over her head. She stepped out of the tub and dried her-

self with the towel and then stuck her hands through the armholes of the T-shirt.

"How long have I been in here?" she asked sleepily.

"Too long." He swung her up into his arms and marched across the hall and tucked her into bed. "Good night, sleeping beauty." He leaned over and kissed the freckles on her nose.

"Elias…"

If he was the man everyone thought he was, he would have climbed into bed with her and the night would have ended on a pleasant note. But would it have been pleasant? He would have been taking advantage of her. And he would never do that. He cared for her, but he wanted more. He just had to figure out what that was. Thinking about it made his head ache or maybe he was just as tired as she was.

MARIBEL WOKE UP at five o'clock, as usual. Something was different, though. Her T-shirt was damp and she couldn't remember coming to bed. Oh, oh, no! She had a flashback of Elias handing her a towel. And then…he kissed her freckles on her face. She was sure of that. Had she…? Had they…? Oh, no.

She quickly dressed and headed for the kitchen to fix breakfast. All the while, she was trying to remember what had happened last night. She'd been tired, but not *that* tired.

Elias walked in as cool as a spring breeze, poured a cup of coffee and leaned against the counter. He didn't seem smug or anything so she just came out and asked, "What happened last night?"

"You fell asleep in the bathtub. That's not safe, you know."

"Elias, don't…" He had helped her last night and she

decided not to get into an argument. "Thank you for helping me."

"My pleasure."

She glared at him and then took the biscuits out of the oven.

"I'll butter those." He reached for a hot pad. Slathering a biscuit with butter, he added, "You know, your body hasn't changed a bit in all these years."

She gritted her teeth. "Yes, it has. I now have stretch marks thanks to your nine-pound son."

"I'll have to take a second look."

She shook her head. "No, you..." Her words trailed off as Chase and Grandpa came into the room.

They had breakfast and went their separate ways. As she parked at the diner, her hand touched her nose. It was strange how she remembered his lips touching it last night. Soft and gentle. Yet evocative and stirring. He'd called her something. *Sleeping beauty.*

Tough and ornery, Elias had said the words and it gave her the warm fuzzies. Good heavens, was she falling in love with him all over again?

By NOON, ELIAS had fixed the hole in the bedroom and had all the bad Sheetrock pulled out. He was measuring to see how much he needed to buy when Grandpa walked in.

"I got something for you, Elias."

"I'm rather busy right now, Grandpa," he replied, as he measured a wall. "I'm trying to figure out how much Sheetrock we'll need."

"Well, you don't have to figure anymore. Come look at my truck."

"What are you talking about?"

Grandpa walked out the door and Chase followed. Elias said a cuss word under his breath and trailed after them.

He stopped short when he saw Grandpa's truck. It was loaded with Sheetrock.

"Where did you get that?"

"Phoenix and Falcon sent it. It was left over from building their houses."

Elias eyed his grandpa. "Did they send it or did you just take it?"

Grandpa slapped him on the back. "Now how would I get it on the truck?"

Good point. The brothers had always helped each other and even though Elias was an outcast, sort of, they still stuck together.

Elias let down the tailgate. "Come on, kid. Let's unload this into the house."

Elias and Chase worked on putting the new Sheetrock up. Maribel came at about 2:30 p.m. and went to work in the spare bathroom, removing the old tile. She worked as hard as he did and he realized they had that in common. She wasn't afraid of work. Their son had those genes, too.

As he worked, he thought of her and last night, all soft and cuddly—dreamlike. He'd always said he'd never get married. Being tied down wasn't for him. Yet, it had been weeks and he hadn't had a drink of beer since he'd found out he was a father. He didn't even have the inclination to go down to Rowdy's. Nor did he have the time. He couldn't figure that one out. He'd lived for his evenings at Rowdy's, talking to the ladies and having fun. Now all he wanted was to spend time with Maribel and Chase. They say you can never be too old to grow up.

He and Chase went outside to get more Sheetrock. Elias froze as he saw Ira McCray drive up. His sons, Gunnar and Malachi, were behind him in another truck. Ira got out with a shotgun in his hand. His sons tried talking to him, but Ira pushed them away and walked toward Elias.

"Go in the house," Elias said to Chase.

"No. I…"

"Go into the house. Now!"

Chase disappeared into the house and the old man confronted Elias. "You raped my daughter and now I'm going to kill you." He pointed the gun at Elias's chest.

Elias flung his arms wide. "Go ahead, Mr. McCray. If it will avenge some of the pain caused by the Rebel/McCray feud, go ahead and fire away. But I have to tell you, there was no rape involved."

Before Ira could pull the trigger, Maribel came storming out of the house with Chase behind her. "What are you doing?" she asked her father.

"This man raped you. That's why you wouldn't tell me who the father was. You knew I'd kill him."

"Oh, please. You're concerned for me now? Eighteen years ago, you kicked me out and I had nowhere to go, so please don't make this about me. Elias and I had consensual sex in high school one time and we both knew it was wrong. It was my choice and I don't regret it. My pregnancy has nothing to do with you or your high moral ground. And I do not appreciate you coming here all indignant on my behalf."

The loud wail of a siren could be heard. Wyatt pulled into the driveway. He jumped out and rushed toward them. He walked straight to Ira and yanked the shotgun from him. "Let's go, Ira, you're trespassing."

"My daughter…" The old man's skin was pasty white and he seemed wobbly.

"Your daughter is fine and no one is harming her. She's where she wants to be and you have to accept that."

"I'm not pressing charges, Wyatt," Elias said. "Let him go."

Wyatt looked perplexed. "Are you sure?"

"We'll make sure he doesn't come back," Gunnar said.

"Mr. McCray, I'm going to let you go, but if you point a gun at someone else, you will spend some time in jail. You've let it go for several years. Don't change that now."

As the McCrays walked off, Maribel shouted, "Wait!"

Gunnar and Malachi stopped and looked back. Her father kept walking.

Maribel reached for Chase and pulled him forward. "I want you to meet someone. This is my son, Chase. And these are your uncles, Gunnar and Malachi."

They shook hands. The kid stood there almost paralyzed with this unexpected development of meeting his new relatives. Chase inched closer to Elias while Maribel talked to her brothers.

Malachi hugged his sister. "It's good to have you home, Maribel. Maybe we could have you out to dinner one night so you can meet my family."

"I'd like that, but it might be too soon."

Malachi glanced toward his father's truck. "I know, but he'll come around. He's just stubborn and clings to the old ways."

The McCray boys walked back to their truck and Maribel went into the house.

"Was Mom crying?" Chase asked.

"I'll go see."

"It's best to leave her alone when she's upset," Chase told him.

"Yeah, that's what a sane person would do."

Maribel was in the spare bathroom, breaking tile with a hammer and throwing it into a bucket.

"Are you okay?"

"Go away, Elias."

"I'm not going anywhere until I know you're okay."

She turned around, her blue eyes blazing. "I just met

my family again for the first time in eighteen years. How do you think that makes me feel? And you? How could you dare my father to shoot you? Did you even think about me and Chase?"

"I just went with the moment, like I always do."

She brushed away her hair with an angry hand. "Sometimes you need to think."

He tilted his head to look into her eyes. "Were you worried about me?"

She laid the hammer on the vanity. "I guess. Chase just got his father back into his life and he could have been gone in a heartbeat."

"Ah, Maribel. You're making my poor ol' heart flutter."

The sadness in her eyes disappeared. "You're crazy."

He winked. "And you love crazy."

"I guess," she hiccupped.

They were the most beautiful words he'd ever heard.

Chapter Eleven

June faded into July and Maribel was happier about her future than she'd ever been. The house was looking great and the mildew smell was gone. She picked out paint colors, tile and bathroom fixtures. It was exciting and she couldn't believe the beautiful house was going to be hers. She went with the color *wheat* for the whole house, but in the master bedroom she'd chosen a barely-green color. It was relaxing and soothing, and she couldn't wait to move in.

Elias was installing the new air-conditioning and heating unit, and his brothers stopped by every now and then to help him lay tile. But Elias really didn't need any help. He was a workhorse and knew how to do everything.

She loved her job at the diner and getting to know the people in Horseshoe again. Her brothers stopped by with their families and she got to meet them on neutral ground and she loved it. Even her twin brothers, Ashton and Axel, brought in their families. They always asked about Rosie and she told them the truth, that she was having a difficult pregnancy. The McCrays were slowly coming back together. But her father stayed away. Oddly, that didn't bother her too much.

She opened the door to the house and a cool breeze embraced her. Elias had the AC on. It was working. She called but no one answered. Looking out the patio window, she

saw Chase on a riding lawn mower with Elias giving him directions. Chase had never mowed a yard and she started to go outside to let Elias know that, but then she stayed where she was, watching.

The mower was a John Deere and worked with levers instead of a steering wheel. Those were difficult to learn, but Chase was getting the hang of it. Just like Elias, he learned easily. Elias walked toward the house and let Chase mow.

His easy confident strides always made her take a second look. That's who Elias was, self-assured and capable. She'd always admired that in him and looking around at the house, she couldn't have admired anyone more. They'd washed all the windows and Elias had taken down all the screens and new ones were being made. Soon the house would be brand-new—because of Elias.

"What do you think?" Elias asked as he came through the door.

"It feels great." She knew he was talking about the AC. It was hot in Texas at this time of year.

"Did you see the kitchen? The backsplash is finished."

She swung around. She was so busy watching Elias she hadn't even looked at the kitchen. "Oh, it's beautiful. Just like the picture I had in my head with the creams, tans and browns. It matches the granite perfectly." She smiled at him. "Thank you."

His eyes met hers for a moment and that old flame sparked between them. She felt as if she was in high school, looking at him across the room and wondering what it would feel like to be kissed by him.

"Paxton came by early this morning and we got the tile down in Chase's bathroom and in the spare bathroom. Tomorrow, the kid and I will work on the kitchen floor."

She clapped her hands. "It's all coming together."

"Yep. I picked up the flooring today and most of it is stacked in the living room." He walked into the living room and ripped open a box. Pulling out a plank of dark wood, he said, "That's what you picked out."

She took the plank from him and ran her hand over the smoothness. "I was afraid it was going to be too dark, but the hickory color goes good in here with the dark trim."

"Yeah." He sat on the floor and leaned back against the wall. "Soon you'll be able to move in."

She eased to the floor, sitting cross-legged. "I can hardly believe it."

"I want to talk to you about something."

A chill ran up her spine. When anyone said those words to her, it meant bad news and she didn't want to hear anything bad today. But he didn't say anything and she wondered if he was going to speak at all. He wiped his hands on his jeans.

"I think a lot about Chase and his being without a father all those years. I'm going to be in his life twenty-four-seven from now on."

"I know. You've made that very clear."

He looked at her then. "Does that bother you?"

She brushed a speck of dirt from her jeans. "Not anymore. You've been very good for Chase. I've seen him change right before my eyes. He respects you."

A crooked grin cracked his stern expression. "We've come a long way in a few weeks and…and I want us to go further."

"What do you mean?"

"I want us to move into this house as a family."

She was confused. "You mean like we're living in Paige's house?"

"No. I want to make it official. I want us to get married and make a real home for Chase."

Marriage!

It took a moment for her heart to stop soaring. Was he serious? From the stern expression on his face she knew he was. When she was a naive teenager, she used to dream of them getting married and living happily ever after. But she was an adult now and this was for real.

She never for one moment thought he would propose to her. Much less on the floor of the house they were remodeling. She supposed it was a proposal. There were no words of love nor did she want them. The emotion was highly overrated.

The proposal sounded perfect for them—no emotions involved. She just had this feeling he was adrift and needed an anchor. She wanted it to be more than that. Why? She couldn't explain.

"Elias, you really need to talk to your mother and smooth over all the hurt and pain and go home to Rebel Ranch. That's where your heart is."

He shook his head. "I thought I would never leave the ranch I loved and grew up on, but lately I haven't thought much about it, nor have I yearned to go back. My place now is with you and Chase. I want us to be a family like we should have been all those years ago. Although, I'm not sure how that would've worked out back then. But I know it can work now."

"Marriage is never a sure thing."

He frowned. "You're resisting this. Why?"

His phone buzzed and she waited for him to answer it. He didn't.

"Aren't you going to see who that is?"

"Nah. It's just one of my brothers."

"Look at it."

Reluctantly, he pulled the phone out of his pocket and stared at a text message.

"Who is it?"

"Bob, from Rowdy's."

Before he could put away his phone, she scooted closer to see the message:

When are you coming back? The ladies are missing you.

"Ladies?" She lifted an eyebrow. "How many women are you seeing?"

He stuffed the phone back into his pocket. "None. And I haven't been to Rowdy's since the night Chase was arrested. I haven't had any beer, either. I'll never drink in front of my son."

"Elias, Chase doesn't care if you drink."

He shrugged. "I don't have the need for it anymore. I know most people thought I was an alcoholic, but I never really drank that much. I just liked going down to the bar and hanging out. Life gets lonely sometimes. And, believe me, I haven't felt lonely in several weeks."

Maribel sank back on her heels, not knowing what to say. Was this Elias? The real rebel in the family? Pouring out his heart like he cared? She glanced around the room and saw all the love he'd put into the house. It was her future. It was his future.

She held out her hand. "Let me see your phone."

He handed it to her with his trademark frown etched on his face.

She texted Bob:

Elias is not coming back unless I'm with him, so tell the ladies to back off.

She tossed the phone back to Elias and he read her message.

His eyes met hers. "Is that a *yes*?"

"On two conditions. One, that you don't expect vows of love."

"O-kay."

"And…"

"What?"

"That Chase approves of the marriage."

"Maribel, he can't even say my name. It will take time for him to accept me. We're the adults and we have to set the rules."

"I know, but I can't just throw something else at him again like the move to Horseshoe. I have to be honest with him and let him have a say on what happens next."

"You're going to put our future in our son's hands."

"Don't you trust him? I do. He's not the same kid who stole beer and ran from the law. He's changed and I want him to feel a part of our future."

Elias got to his feet in one swift movement. "Okay, let's do this."

They walked out to the patio and sat on the step, watching their son as he circled the backyard with the lawn mower. He made the last round and stopped the mower about six feet from them. He jumped off and brushed his brow with the back of his hand.

"What's up? Why are y'all sitting out here?"

"Go get something to drink," Maribel told him. "You look hot." Sweat stained his shirt and shorts.

"This isn't going to be easy," she said to Elias as Chase walked off.

"Do you want me to do the talking?"

She shook her head. "No. I'm his mother and I need to do it."

Chase came back with a bottle of water in his hand. "What's up?" he asked again.

"We want to talk to you."

"About what?" He took a long drink of water. "I know I haven't done anything wrong so it must be that you've decided to buy me that red Silverado down at Bubba's garage."

"It's not about the truck," Elias said.

"Dang." Chase sat on the lawn mower, and placed the bottle of water beside him.

"We'd like to talk to you."

"Sure." He glanced at them with big brown eyes.

Maribel wasn't sure where to start, as she looked into his trusting eyes. She cleared her throat. "Your father and I have been talking."

"About me?"

"Mostly about us, but it includes you." She glanced at Elias. "We're talking about getting married and moving into the house as a family and we'd like to know how you feel about that."

An Elias-frown marred his face and Maribel held her breath. "You mean like man-and-wife?"

"Yes, son," Elias said. "We want to make a home for you as you go into your senior year and off to college."

"Aren't you supposed to be in love or something?"

Maribel linked her arm through Elias's. "We feel very deeply for each other and we always have. We feel this union is right for all of us."

Chase slid off the lawn mower. "I mean…Billy Tom and Brandon have fathers and…well…if you really want… I mean he is my father. He's my real father. He's my father. He's my father." Chase couldn't stop saying the words over and over and Maribel's heart stopped at her son's obvious distress.

Before she could move, Elias got to his feet and went to his son. "That's who I am—your father. And that's never going to change. I'm always going to be here for you,

looking over your shoulder, supporting you, loving you. That's who I am."

Chase brushed away a tear. "You're my father."

"Yes." Elias enveloped him in a big hug and Chase wrapped his arms around Elias's waist and cried into his chest. Maribel hadn't seen him cry in a long time. She went to them and wrapped her arms around the two.

"We're a family," she said, pushing past the wad in her throat.

Chase raised his head. "Yes, we're a family. A real family, and we're going to move into this house as a family."

"Yes, we are." Maribel smiled. It had gone better than she'd ever expected, but she knew her son admired Elias. It was just a matter of time before he admitted it.

Grandpa came out the patio door. "What's everyone doing out here where it's hot?"

Chase ran to him. "Guess what, Grandpa? Mom and—" he glanced at Elias "—Dad are getting married."

At the word, Elias's heart almost pounded out of his chest.

"You don't say."

"That's better than red-eye gravy on a biscuit, right?"

"Right." Grandpa grinned.

Chase jumped on the mower. "I have to mow the front yard. I'm getting really good at this, Grandpa. You have to come watch."

"I'll be out there in a minute," Grandpa said. "I need to talk to your parents first."

Chase cranked up the mower and off he went.

There was something in Mr. Abe's voice that bothered Maribel. He wasn't as happy as she'd thought he would have been.

"I'm real happy about you two. It's about time to make this legal, but Elias, I think you have to make things right

with your mother first. I know you think I'm the last person who would say that. She hasn't been the same lately, though. She stays in the house and doesn't join the boys in the hay fields like she used to. She's made a mistake and she can't admit it. You need to talk to your mother. You have to be the one to bend. I'm sorry. That's just the way it is. I wouldn't ask this of you, but she's not looking good. I saw her this morning and she was very pale and I don't think she's eating. I know John wouldn't want this. I'd be the first one not to bend to Kate Rebel. I'm just worried, son. Something has to be done."

She watched Elias's face. He stood there strong as any oak, nothing showing on his face but strength and determination. "I'm sure she's fine, Grandpa. We have to deal with this in our own way."

"You love that ranch," Grandpa kept on. "It's struggling right now because you're not there. There's hay in the field and more to be baled. It's going to be a big loss to lose a crop of hay. At least think about helping your brothers. They need you."

"They'll do fine," Elias replied. "I have work to do."

"You're as stubborn as your father."

Elias patted his grandpa's shoulder. "That's where I got it."

Maribel followed Elias into the house. "I don't want to interfere, but shouldn't you think about what your grandfather said."

"I can't go home until my mother asks me to come back. Can't you understand that?"

The pain in his voice made her heart skip a beat. She'd never seen him so emotional unless it was about Chase. "Elias." She stepped closer to him. "It's your mother. Be the bigger person. Take the first step to heal this rift within your family. What kind of life can we build on sadness?"

He threw up his hands. "Don't try to fix this. You just don't understand."

"I understand. You had to leave because of me and Chase. I understand that. I lived with the Rebel/McCray feud all my life. It's time to put it to rest. If you make the first step, your mother will meet you halfway. I just know that."

"You don't know that. You're sticking your nose in something that doesn't concern you."

That revved up her blood pressure. "If I'm marrying you, it's my business."

"So you're changing your mind?"

"I didn't say that. I'm saying you love that ranch and I know you miss it. It's time to think about talking to your mother."

He removed his straw hat in anger and roughly threw it with a strong hand. It landed somewhere in the living room. "I'll think about it. Okay?"

He leaned against the new granite countertop and she went to him and wrapped her arms around his waist, resting her head on his chest. It was the first time she'd willingly touched him. There were so many times she'd wanted to, but today she needed to.

"I'll be here and so will Chase."

His arms tightened around her and they stood there holding on to each other, knowing their past and their futures were entwined in ways that could never be undone.

Elias's phone buzzed and Maribel stepped back. "Aren't you going to answer it?"

He shook his head. "No. It's just one of my brothers with the same message as Grandpa."

Maribel took the phone out of his pocket and looked at it. "It's Quincy." She handed it back to him. "Answer it. It's not a text."

"Maribel…"

"We can handle this."

With a sigh, he clicked on and she watched as the blood drained from his face.

"What is it?"

"My mother… My mother just had a heart attack."

Chapter Twelve

The ride to the hospital was made in silence. Elias broke the speed limit but he didn't care. He had to get to his mother. Every mile, he kept thinking it was all his fault.

Maribel sat on the passenger side and Chase and Grandpa were in the back seat. Maribel had his phone and was giving him updates.

"The ambulance just pulled into the ER and they're unloading her," Maribel read from Quincy's text. "She still not conscious."

"Tell him we'll be there in less than five minutes."

Elias pulled in to the parking lot with a lump in his throat. He found Falcon's truck and parked beside it. He got out and grabbed Maribel's hand and ran for the ER. Chase and Grandpa followed more slowly. Since his father's death, he'd never needed anyone, but today he needed Maribel to get through this.

They went through the automatic glass doors and saw Falcon and Quincy standing to the left.

"What happened?" Elias asked.

From his brothers' pale faces, he knew it was bad.

"We were in the office, just Mom and me," Falcon said. "I told her we needed more help to get the hay in and she said to do whatever I wanted. Then she grabbed her chest and fell to the floor. It's a sight I'll never forget." Falcon

turned away and then turned back. "What the hell is taking so long?"

His other brothers came running in, dirty from the hay fields. "How's Mom?" Egan asked.

"We don't know," Quincy said. "They're working on her. The paramedic felt it was either a heart attack or a stroke. We just have to wait."

His brothers milled around, waiting, but they were all glancing at him and he knew what they were thinking: *It's your fault.* But no one said it out loud.

A nurse came up to them. "There's a waiting room to the right," she said and they all filed into the small room. Grandpa sank into a chair as white as Elias had ever seen him. Chase stayed close to Grandpa. Elias's chest felt like a forty-pound bowling ball was sitting on it and he was having trouble breathing. He gripped Maribel's hand tighter.

His brothers paced. Some sat and then they got back up again. They were all worried. A coldness settled over Elias and a chill touched his soul. How would he survive if something happened to his mother? There was no going back, though, and he had to face this head-on. He stood a little taller and a little bolder. His mom would want him to.

A doctor in scrubs came into the waiting room. "Rebel family?"

They all went to meet him.

The doctor raised an eyebrow. "You're all with Kate Rebel?"

"We're her sons," Falcon said. "How's our mom?"

Elias held his breath as he waited for the next words because he knew they would stay with him for the rest of his life.

"Your mom did not have a heart attack or a stroke. She had an anxiety attack and she's resting comfortably now."

Everyone sagged with relief.

"What does this mean?" Quincy asked.

"It means she's been under a lot of stress and now she's going to have to take it easy and I'm counting on all of you to make that happen."

"Yes, sir," echoed around the room.

"We're going to keep her for a few days to monitor her and we're going to limit visitation. Only two people at a time. The main thing for her right now is to keep her quiet and relaxed. We'll be taking her up to a room in a few minutes. All of you can go home and sort through visiting times. I'm serious—only two people at a time. But she's asking to see Elias. Which one is Elias?"

Elias raised his hand. "That's me."

"I'll allow you ten minutes with her. Agree with whatever she tells you. Don't upset her."

He swallowed hard. "I won't."

The doctor walked away.

Falcon turned to Elias. "Do exactly as he says."

"I wouldn't think of doing anything else, Falcon."

"You and Mom have to sort this out, but not tonight."

He didn't want to get into an argument with his brothers. He turned around and wrapped his arm around Maribel. His legs were wobbly and he needed her to hold on to.

She patted his chest. "Your mom's okay. Everything's going to be fine."

He drew a deep breath and blinked back a tear. "I know. I can hardly believe it. And you were right. I should have talked to her before now."

"Since we can't see her, I guess we need to get back to work," Egan said.

"That's a good idea," Falcon added. "I'll put a schedule in the office in the morning for visiting times. I'll check with the doctor first. She's going to be okay. That's the main thing."

"I don't think she's going to want to see anybody but Elias for the next few days." Phoenix slapped Elias on the shoulder.

"That's probably true." Quincy joined his brothers as they left the hospital.

Chase came to Elias's side. "Dad, Grandpa is shaky and he can't get up."

Dad. It sounded so beautiful in that moment in time.

Elias went to his grandpa in the waiting room and sat beside him. "How you doing?"

"Could you get me something to eat or drink?"

"I'll get it," Chase said and turned toward a vending machine. He quickly turned back. "I don't have any money."

Elias pulled out his wallet and handed Chase a couple of bills. "Get something for yourself, too, and see if your mom wants something."

"Grandpa, Mom's going to be okay so you can stop worrying. But you and Maribel were right. I should've gone home a long time ago. Just can't escape from being stubborn."

Grandpa slapped him on the leg. "It's in your DNA."

Chase handed Grandpa a Coke and some peanut butter crackers.

Maribel sat beside him, drinking a soda.

A nurse came into the room. "Your mother is in her room and she's asking for you."

Elias got to his feet. "Thanks."

"We'll wait for you here," Maribel said.

He shook his head. "No, I need you with me." Admitting that meant some of the stubbornness in him had been chipped away.

Chase stayed with Grandpa and he and Maribel took the elevator up to his mother's room. He met another doctor who once again cautioned him about upsetting his mother.

"It'll be okay, Elias," Maribel told him. "She wants to see you for a reason. And it's a good reason."

Elias held on to that thought as he pushed the door open. The moment he saw his mother lying in the bed so pale and lifeless, his heart fell to the pit of his stomach. An IV was in one arm and she was hooked up to a heart monitor. He had never seen her look so pale. The beep of the monitor sounded like an alarm going off in his head. For a moment, he couldn't move as he realized how much his mother had aged.

The moment she saw him, she held out her hand. "Elias, Elias, come here."

He immediately went to the bedside and she reached for his hand and gripped it with more strength than he thought she had.

"I'm sorry. I'm so sorry." Her words were weak and almost breathless. "I would never disinherit you. Please believe that."

He swallowed hard. "I do, Mom."

"I can't believe I said that."

"It's okay, Mom. Everything's okay."

She shook her head. "No, it's not. I did a terrible thing. A horrible thing. I will never be able to forgive myself."

He gripped her hand. "I forgive you, Mom."

"You shouldn't. Your father must be so upset with me. He used to say I was the most stubborn woman he'd ever met and he was right. I just couldn't admit what I'd done. Sending our first male grandson away to live who knows what kind of life."

"Maribel did okay, Mom. She was helped by a woman named Miss Vennie, who was like a mother to her and a grandmother to Chase. They had a good life until Maribel lost her job."

"I'm glad someone was there for them." She squeezed Elias's hand. "I want to tell you what happened that day."

"You don't have to."

"That morning I couldn't wake your dad. He'd been drinking all night and was out like a light. He didn't even go to work, which was unusual. I was angry at what the McCrays had done to our lives and then Maribel showed up, saying she was pregnant with your child. I just knew it was Ira's way of getting back at us. To make us suffer. Not for one minute did I believe she was telling the truth." A tear slipped from his mother's eyes. "I'm so sorry."

"There's no need to be. I understand how you felt. I understand what was going on at the time and so does Maribel. For all our sakes, just let it go."

"I have to see her, Elias. I won't have any peace until I see Maribel."

"The doctor said you had to rest and you can't have visitors."

His mom looked at the nurse standing on the other side of the bed. "I need to see my doctor. I have to talk to him."

"Mrs. Rebel, you have to rest."

"I won't get any rest until I see this young woman and her son…my grandson."

"I'll see if he's still at the nurse's station." The nurse left the room and Elias wasn't sure what to say.

In a minute, the nurse was back. "The doctor said for only a minute and he's ordered another medication so you can rest. So make it quick."

Elias went into the hall to get Maribel, who had her own doubts.

"Elias, I don't think this is wise."

"Me, either. But she's insisting and the doctor said it was okay." They went back-and-forth but Elias knew he had to do what his mother wanted. Chase was opposed to

seeing his grandmother. But after more discussion, Elias walked back into the room with Maribel and his son behind him. He planned to make it short.

Before he could say anything, his mother held out her hand, "Maribel, please come closer."

Maribel walked to the bedside.

"I'm so sorry for the way I have treated you. I will never get over the injustice I have done to you and your son. Please forgive me. I'm just a crazy old woman, clinging to a past that has died long ago."

"It's okay, Miss Kate," Maribel said. "Just get well again. That's what we want."

"You're so nice." His mother's eyes glanced toward the door where Chase was standing like a statue. "Can I please meet my grandson? I know I don't deserve to, but I'm begging you."

Elias put his hand on Chase's back and slowly moved him forward. "Mom, this is my son, Chase."

"Oh." Another tear slipped from his mother's eyes. "You look so much like your father and your grandfather. Elias is more like his father than any of my sons. He has that stubborn streak in him and his work ethics are the same as John's. I'm so sorry you never got to meet your grandfather and he would be so angry with me for the choices I made when your mother came to the house. Please forgive me."

Chase cleared his throat. "It's okay. My mom took good care of me and so did Nana."

"I'm glad. I hope someday you'll accept me as your grandma."

The nurse injected something into the IV. "Visiting time is over, Mrs. Rebel. You can see your family again tomorrow."

Elias leaned over and kissed his mother's forehead. "Get

some rest and I'll be back tomorrow. Just don't worry about anything."

"Elias." She reached up and touched his face and a warmth shot through him as if he was five years old again. "They need you on the ranch. They need your help to get the hay in. Think about coming home, please."

He swallowed the tightness in his throat. "I will. And don't worry."

Elias walked out of the hospital with his family and for the first time he felt as if he and Maribel and Chase were a family. And, of course, Grandpa. It was a surreal moment.

As he got into his truck, he knew when he'd told his mother he would think about coming back to the ranch that he would. His mother knew it, too. He would have to burn the candle at both ends and then some. But never again would he disappoint the women in his life: his mother and Maribel.

MARIBEL WANTED TO say something on the drive home, but felt it was better if she remained silent. Elias had a lot on his mind. She was just happy Miss Kate was going to be okay.

As soon as they reached the house, Elias went to work, laying the flooring in Chase's bedroom. He'd had no plans to do that today but she didn't question him. It was late, so she went to Paige's house to cook supper. Grandpa went with her. He was exhausted and fell asleep on the sofa.

Chase came in at about eight o'clock.

"Where's your father?"

"He's still working. He told me to go home and eat. I told him I'd stay, but he said in that deep no-nonsense voice to go home, so I did."

At ten o'clock, Elias still wasn't home. Chase and Grandpa were asleep, so she got in her car and went back

to the house in her T-shirt and flip-flops. Elias was laying the flooring in the study. He already had the flooring finished in the two bedrooms.

"Elias, it's time to quit."

He swabbed glue onto the floor and laid a hard wood plank in place and tapped it to fit securely. "As soon as I finish the study, I'll be home."

"You're coming home now. The flooring can wait."

"Maribel…"

"Now, Elias. We have plenty of time to get the flooring in, but not at the risk of your health."

Surprisingly, he got to his feet. But he winced.

"What's wrong?"

"Nothing, just a little stiff from being on my knees."

She hooked an arm around his waist. "Let's go home."

At the house, he quickly ate supper, took a shower and fell into bed. When she went to check on him, he was sprawled on the king-size bed on his stomach in his underwear.

"Are you okay?"

"Yeah. Just tired."

"Does your back hurt?"

"A little."

For him to admit that, she knew it must hurt a lot.

"Did you know that I give a killer massage?" She straddled his back and started to knead the tight muscles in his shoulders.

"Ah, Mari, I think I'm dreaming."

She loved it when he called her that. It came out *Merry.*

"I'll be working on the house and helping with the hay, too. I'll take Chase with me."

She had known that was his intention by his sudden mad rush to finish the house that evening. "Elias, just take it slow." His muscles were tight and she continued to

rub until she felt him relax. Touching the strong muscles of his back was intimate and tempting. It had been a long time since she'd touched him and she wanted to continue to touch him long into the night. The thought stopped her hands.

Elias reached around with one arm and pulled her down beside him. "Sleep with me tonight, Mari."

Without thinking about it, she snuggled into his almost naked frame and felt alive for the first time since she was seventeen years old. It wouldn't hurt to stay here for a few minutes just to enjoy being with him. She didn't question her motive. She just went with her feelings.

When she awoke at 5:00 a.m. the spot beside her was empty and a loneliness crept into her soul. She knew Elias wasn't in the bathroom. There was only one place he'd go at this time of the morning: the hospital.

He'd gone to see his mother.

And the loneliness grew deeper.

Chapter Thirteen

The next morning, Elias crawled out of bed reluctantly. The sight of Maribel lying there with her hair all over the pillow and her long smooth legs visible from under the T-shirt made him pause. He just wanted to crawl back in bed and spend the rest of the day with her.

But duty called.

He checked in on his mom and she was much better and ready to go home. She looked like her old self and his heart eased. He told her he would be helping with the hay and that made her feel even better. She apologized all over again and he didn't want a repeat of yesterday so he told her he had to go.

Back at the house he had a quick breakfast then he, Chase and Grandpa went to work. Grandpa sat in a chair watching them lay the flooring in the study and the master bedroom. At eight o'clock, they headed to Rebel Ranch.

Elias knew the schedule during hay months. First thing in the morning, they took care of the cattle and the horses and then met at the office to discuss the rest of the day. The office was full by the time they got there.

Falcon was speaking but stopped when they entered the room. "Welcome back, Elias."

He nodded. "I'd like everyone to meet my son, Chase. I didn't get to do that yesterday with all the excitement."

Chase shook hands with his uncles. Zane, Jude's almost sixteen-year-old son, walked up to Chase.

"I'm Zane."

"So?"

Elias didn't like the attitude, but he didn't say anything. He knew his son was nervous meeting so many people at one time.

"I'm your cousin. You're living in my mom's house."

"Oh. Thanks."

His son was at a loss for words. Zane was a good kid and Elias knew the two boys would work it out on their own.

"Okay, well…" Falcon got back to business. "Quincy will be bailing today and Jude and Egan will be working on the second hay baler, which broke yesterday. We have hundreds of round bales that need to be taken off the field. And we have one thousand alfalfa bales on the field, too. Mr. Whitaker wants five hundred alfalfa bales delivered to his farm today. Mr. Cummings is coming with his trailer to be loaded with two hundred bales at one o'clock and Mr. Dorsey is coming at three with his trailer to be loaded with two hundred bales. That leaves one hundred bales on the field that need to go into the barn. Pick your poison."

"Jericho and I will take care of the alfalfa bales," Elias said.

"You mean the bales to Mr. Whitaker?" Falcon asked.

"No. I mean I'll take care of the alfalfa bales to everyone."

Falcon sighed. "You can't do all that in one day, Elias."

"Do you know me, Falcon?"

Falcon sighed. "Okay. But call me if you can't load Mr. Cummings's trailer. I'll need to alert him and Mr. Dorsey."

"There'll be no phone call." Elias turned to Rico. "Ready?"

"Ready."

"Since Dad is working on the baler, I'll help Uncle Elias today," Zane said.

"You got it, kid." Elias put an arm around his nephew.

"That leaves Paxton and Phoenix to move round bales with the tractors to the fence rows." Falcon got to his feet. "And I'm on my way to the hospital."

"I was there this morning," Elias told them. "And she's doing fine. She's getting antsy to come home."

"I was there, too," Quincy added.

"Me, too," echoed around the room and then they all laughed.

"How did we miss each other?" Egan asked.

"I guess we're all good at being sneaky." Phoenix headed for the door. "Let's go, Pax. We have hay to move."

Elias hooked up a three-quarter ton company truck to a long flatbed trailer. Afterward, he said to his small group, "This is how it's going to go. Grandpa is going to drive the truck. Rico and I will throw the bales onto the trailer and Chase and Zane will stack them."

Zane pointed to Chase. "He's going to get his legs all scratched up in shorts."

"I can wear what I want," Chase shot back.

Elias took a long breath. "Son, I don't have time for attitude today. Zane is right and I should've realized it before now, but shorts are not appropriate for hauling hay."

"He's about my size and he can wear some of my clothes," Zane offered.

"I'm not wearing his clothes."

Elias took another long breath. "As I said, I don't have time for this today. Go with Zane and pick out some clothes and let's get to work."

"Do I have to?"

"Yes, son, you have to."

"They'll work it out," Rico said.

"Yeah." But Elias had his doubts.

Ten minutes later they headed for the hay field. Chase was sullen at first, but then he and Zane got to talking and things got better. Elias had wanted to show his son the ranch, but he wouldn't have time for that today.

When they got there, Grandpa took the driver's seat and Elias and Rico started throwing bales of hay onto the trailer, one on each side. But they had one problem: Chase wasn't sure what to do.

"Plant your feet slightly apart and bend you knees. Reach for the strings on the bale and lift, straightening your knees while keeping your back straight. Stack the bales at the front of the trailer. Two high and then we'll stack more on top of that until we have two hundred and fifty bales on this trailer. Watch Zane and you'll learn. You have to be quick because Rico and I will be quick. You have to keep up."

"Uncle Elias taught me," Zane spoke up.

Elias jumped from the trailer. "Let's do it."

It took a while for Chase to catch on and it slowed them down. Chase wasn't going to have Zane outdo him, though, and by the time they had the first layer of bales on the trailer, Chase had it down. They delivered the hay to Mr. Whitaker and were back at the house by noon. They were just getting started.

As they headed back to the hay field, he got a text from Maribel.

Where are you? I have lunch.

Ah, he knew there was a reason he loved that woman. *Loved.* He hadn't thought about it much since they'd talked about marriage. He had never felt about anyone the way

he felt about her. But for now, everything was on hold and he hated that. He hated to put her second.

He turned the truck around and met her. She jumped out of the car and handed him two small ice chests. "One is cold. One is hot. I'll see you tonight. I have to go. I'm on my break."

They ate lunch under a big oak tree and then they got back to work. At five o'clock, they still had the last two hundred and fifty bales to deliver to Mr. Whitaker. Grandpa said it was time to quit, but Elias wouldn't hear of it. It would just be more work to do tomorrow. It was nine o'clock when he finally drove the truck and trailer into the equipment shed. Everyone was tired and dirty.

Falcon met them. "How much more hay is on the field? Rain is expected in a couple of days."

"None."

"What?"

Elias removed his hat and wiped his dusty brow. "I told you I'd do it and it's done. Now I'm going home with my kid."

"Man, I'm glad you're back, Elias."

Rico fell into step beside him. "You coming back tomorrow?"

"You bet, so get some rest. We'll do it all over again tomorrow."

Rico patted him on the shoulder. "I'm glad you're home. It's just not the same without you."

Home. That's where Maribel was and for the first time he felt torn between home and family and Maribel. But he knew where his heart was: with Maribel.

CHASE AND GRANDPA came in at ten o'clock and ate supper. She didn't even ask where Elias was because she knew he

was probably working on the house or at the hospital. He would come in later.

That set the pattern for the next two weeks. She rarely saw Elias except when she rubbed his back late at night and helped him to relax. But she made sure she went back to her own room. She would lie awake and wonder if he remembered proposing to her and what his plans were about marriage. Since she wasn't that fond of love and marriage, she wasn't sure what she was worried about or what was annoying her.

Miss Kate came home from the hospital and was back to her old self, carrying lunch to her sons while they worked. Toward the end of July, Paige gave birth to a baby girl named Olivia. They were calling her Livy. All work came to a halt so everyone could go and see the baby. Rosie was still on bed rest and while Elias and Chase worked, she got to spend more time with her sister.

Phoenix and Paxton helped Elias finish the flooring and tile in the house. They couldn't walk on the floors for twenty-four hours so Maribel headed to Temple to buy clothes for Chase. She bought some Wrangler jeans for him to work in, but he needed clothes for school, too. "Wrangler jeans, Mom," was all she heard. Her son was becoming a cowboy—just like his father.

She bought sheets, comforters, dishes, silverware, pots and pans, and blinds for every room in the new house. She wanted Elias to go with her to shop for furniture, but she wasn't sure when that would be.

Walking through the department store, she stopped in the women's clothing area. On a mannequin was a white eyelet calf-length dress that caught her attention. It had spaghetti straps and the bodice fit tight and flared out around the hips. The mannequin also wore a white floppy hat. It was a perfect summer outfit. Perfect enough for a

wedding if she believed in fairytales, which she didn't. So she couldn't explain why she bought the dress. Maybe she was catching what Elias had—a little bit of crazy.

JULY WAS BUSY and Elias barely had time to catch his breath. Chase had finished his community service and Wyatt had called Elias and said he was proud of Chase and the young man he was becoming. That made Elias feel good.

When Elias got home, Chase was sprawled on the sofa. Pushing Chase's legs aside, he sat by his son. "Wyatt called and you're a free man again. You did a good job. I'm proud of you."

"Thanks, Dad." Chase just lay there like he was stunned or something.

"What's wrong with you?"

"I'm in love."

That startled Elias. "With who?"

Chase sat up. "When I finished today, Billy Tom and Brandon met me at the sheriff's office. We wanted to apologize to the sheriff as a group for being stupid. There were two girls there, Erin and Jody. They knew Billy Tom and Brandon and they started talking and then they introduced me. She has the most beautiful eyes I've ever seen in my whole life. They're brown, but they have like green flecks in them. Everything about her is gorgeous."

"Back up. Who are we talking about?"

"Jody. Aren't you listening?"

"What's her last name?"

Chase shrugged. "I don't know. I didn't ask. We talked about school. She and Erin are cheerleaders. I just loved watching her talk."

"Did you even wonder what she was doing in the sheriff's office?"

Chase frowned. "I'm almost sure she wasn't arrested or anything."

Elias rubbed his son's shoulder. "Son, Jody is Jody Carson, as in Wyatt Carson, the sheriff. She's the sheriff's daughter."

Chase shook his head. "No way."

Elias nodded, hoping to get through to his son. No way would Wyatt let Chase date his daughter. Elias knew that for fact.

"Erin, the other girl, is Hardy Hollister's daughter, the DA. They're best friends. I know Jude has taken Zane and Erin to parties so I think Erin is taken."

"I'm not interested in Erin."

"Well, then you better get those love bugs out of your eyes. There are a lot of pretty girls in Horseshoe, but Jody Carson is not the girl for you."

"Dad!"

Elias went into the kitchen where Maribel was putting supper on the table. "You're home early tonight."

"All the hay is off the fields so we decided to quit early. Quincy and Jude will start bailing again tomorrow." Elias looked around. "Where's Grandpa?"

"He said he's eating at Quincy's tonight."

"Since the situation with Mom and me has been resolved, I am hoping he'll go back to his house. I think he was afraid I'd leave town."

She leaned against the counter, her blue eyes sparkling just the way he loved.

"I'll make a bet with you. I bet Grandpa lives with us most of the time from here on out."

"Oh, no." Elias ran his hands up his face. "Grandpa has his own house and that's where he should be."

"He's lonely, Elias."

He eyed her closely, thinking no one could be more

understanding. "And you're okay with Grandpa living with us?"

"He loves our son and our son loves him, so no, I don't have a problem with him living with us."

"You know, if our son wasn't in the other room, I'd jump your bones."

She turned from the stove with an impish light in her eyes. "You don't have enough energy for that."

He started toward her. "I'll show you how much…"

The back door opened and Grandpa walked in. "I'm back."

Elias sighed. "Grandpa, I don't like you driving at night."

"I drive whenever I want to," Grandpa shot back. "Where's the kid?"

"In the living room."

Grandpa stomped off to find Chase. "What's wrong with you?" Elias and Maribel heard him say.

"I'm in love, Grandpa."

"Love? A bumblebee must have stung you, that's all."

Elias glanced at Maribel and he could see she was trying hard not to laugh. He was, too. Grandpa's no-nonsense approach to love was hilarious. He grabbed Maribel and danced her around the kitchen. "I have a lot of energy left. Later, Mari."

BUT LATER NEVER came. Chase and Grandpa were in bed and so was Elias. Maribel was the last to shower and she quickly hurried to her room. Elias was on his stomach in the king-size bed and she didn't think he was awake. So it gave her time to escape, although she wasn't sure what she wanted to escape from.

She didn't want to start their married life until they were legally married. It was old-fashioned, she realized,

and naive when every time she looked at him her hormones went into overdrive. She applied lotion to her arms and her legs and wondered what to do next. She could walk across the hall and she knew what would happen. But her son's bedroom was right there and that held her back. She had to be the adult.

As she pulled back the comforter, her phone buzzed. She glanced at it on the nightstand. Phoenix. She immediately clicked on.

"Maribel, Rosie's bleeding and we're waiting on an ambulance. The doctor said not to move her until the paramedics reached us. I'm scared she's losing the baby. She's asking for you."

"I'll meet you at the hospital."

"I hear the ambulance. We'll be on our way in just a few minutes."

"Where's Jake?"

"Leah's picking him up."

Maribel hurriedly slipped into jeans and flip-flops and ran across to Elias's room. "I'm going to the hospital. The ambulance just picked up Rosie."

Elias was out of bed in a heartbeat and pulled on his jeans. "I'm going with you."

She didn't have time to argue.

"What's going on?" Grandpa asked from the doorway in his boxer shorts and a T-shirt.

"The ambulance picked up Rosie. Phoenix is afraid she's losing the baby."

"Then we need to go the hospital," Grandpa said.

In less than five minutes, they were in the truck and heading for Temple. Chase was still half asleep and putting on his sneakers.

Elias broke the speed limit and they made it to the ER before the ambulance. They saw it as it pulled in and Ma-

ribel jumped from the truck and ran to her sister. She lay so pale on the stretcher and blood had soaked through the sheets. Maribel's breath caught in her throat. *Please, don't let her lose this baby.*

"Maribel." Rosie reached for her as soon as she saw her. She clasped her sister's hand. "I'm scared."

She kissed her sister's forehead. "I know, sweetie, but everything is going to be okay. Just stay strong. I'm right here if you need me. I'm not going anywhere."

"I love you, Mari."

This was when she was supposed to tell her sister she loved her, too. But the words stuck in her throat. If she said them she just knew something bad would happen to the baby and Rosie. As much as she tried, she couldn't push that feeling down. "Me, too, sweetie." She kissed her sister one more time as they rolled the stretcher into the ER with Phoenix behind them.

She stood there in the warm summer night, trembling as if the temperature was freezing. How could she not say the words? What was wrong with her? She wrapped her arms around herself and wondered how one person could get so screwed up. Love was just one of those things she had a hard time dealing with. But Rosie knew she loved her. That's the only thing that gave her comfort.

Elias walked up. "You okay?"

She turned into the circle of his arms, needing comfort like she never had before. "I'm just praying she doesn't lose the baby."

His arms tightened around her and then they walked into the ER to wait. Elias, Grandpa and Chase sat in chairs, but Maribel couldn't sit. She was too nervous. Too angry with herself.

Phoenix came out in scrubs. "They're taking her up to

surgery. The baby is in distress and they're going to do a C-section."

"So the baby's okay?" Maribel asked.

"So far. Just keep praying." He told them where they could go to wait and they took the elevator in silence. No one knew what to say. The night could be a very long one.

Chase brought everybody coffee. Then he and Grandpa fell asleep in their chairs. Elias grabbed her hand and pulled her down beside him.

"Everything's going to be okay. I just feel it."

"I…"

Suddenly, Phoenix came around the corner with a big smile on his face and she knew everything was okay.

"Rosie's fine and the baby's fine. We have a five-pound baby girl and the doctor said even though she's four weeks early, she's fine." Phoenix took a long breath. "Everyone is fine." His knees buckled and Elias caught him.

"Whoa. You better sit down."

"No, I have to get back. Rosie wanted to make sure one of us touched her the moment she was born, so they let me hold her right away. She has these tiny tuffs of red hair. She's gorgeous. Here, look. The nurse took pictures." He showed his phone to Maribel.

She stared at the naked baby and thought she'd never seen anything more beautiful. "She looks like Rosie."

"Yeah. My two redhead angels." He shoved his phone back into his pocket. "Thanks, guys, for being here. It meant a lot to Rosie and me."

"I'm going home to change clothes and I'll call Gladys to take the day off so I can be here for Rosie."

"Thank you, Maribel. She's going to want you here."

Phoenix hurried back into the OR and Elias slipped an arm around her waist. "Everything's okay."

"Yes." She let out a long breath and gave thanks for

the miracle. She leaned against Elias and wondered if she would ever be able to tell him how she felt about him. Or would her feelings stay locked inside where they had been for years? Would her fears keep her from living a full life?

Chapter Fourteen

July faded into August and life got even busier. Maribel signed Chase up for school and he was ready to go. He would start football practice in a week. He and Zane were also becoming fast friends. She had been informed that she didn't need to take Chase to school because Zane would be picking him up in a brand-new truck he was getting for his sixteenth birthday. She was planning to buy Chase a truck for his eighteenth birthday. She needed to talk to Elias, but she rarely saw him and when she did there were other people around.

She'd spent two days and two nights with Rosie when the baby came home. Rosie was nervous, but once she got the hang of it she was fine and so was Phoenix. The thing that surprised Maribel was that she missed being with Elias, Chase and Grandpa. They were her family and she just wanted to go home to them. That's where her heart was.

They had dinner twice at Miss Kate's and everything went smoothly. They'd gone to see the new baby Livy and Miss Kate insisted they stay. They had a good time and Maribel was able to relax. Then Quincy and Jenny's new baby girl, Bailey Rose, was born and they went to see her and had supper at Miss Kate's again. It was like they were

married. But they weren't. At this point, she didn't know if they ever would be. Life just went on.

Since Elias and Chase were busy, she decided to put up the blinds in the house. That was the last thing to be done besides the trim around the hardwood floors. When she drove into the driveway, she saw Elias's truck. She had no idea what he was doing here in the early afternoon.

As she opened the door, she heard hammering. Elias was in the living room, tacking down the trim around the floor. He had on clean jeans and a shirt, and he'd showered and shaved. What was he up to?

"What are you doing here?"

"Finishing the house. I hung the blinds and now I'm finishing the trim. This house is ready to move into."

"Oh."

He tacked a piece of trim in place. "I was thinking when I finish we could go to Temple and buy furniture."

"Oh. I'd like that." He hadn't forgotten.

He rose to his feet and placed the hammer into a toolbox. "We have a budget and we have to stick to it."

"Really? I thought I could just buy willy-nilly."

He glanced at her. "Don't be smart. I get enough of that from our son."

Maribel looked around. "Where is he, by the way?"

"He's with Zane. I gave him the afternoon off and he and Zane are going to do something fun. And by fun, I mean likely hanging around Erin and Jody, I'm sure."

"He's stuck on her."

Elias picked up the toolbox. "Yeah. Just wait until Wyatt finds out and then I might have to deck the sheriff."

"My son is good enough for the sheriff's daughter," she said a little testier than she'd intended.

"Exactly. Isn't it good we think alike?"

She lifted an eyebrow. "Not exactly."

He threw an arm around her shoulder with a cockamamy grin. "Come on, Maribel. Let's go shopping. And believe me, those are words I thought I would never say to a woman."

And shop they did. They agreed on just about everything except the sofa for the living room. She wanted a smaller sofa and Elias wanted a large leather sectional with a recliner in it. She compromised by getting her own comfy chair with a footstool.

It surprised her that she wasn't the one to blow the budget. Elias was. He insisted on a big screen TV for the living room, their room and Chase's room. The argument was Chase was going to play football and Elias wanted to watch him on a big-screen TV. How could she argue with that? So they went over their budget. But Elias didn't seem to mind. The store would deliver the furniture and appliances on Thursday.

Maribel had never had a home of her own and she could hardly contain her excitement. She and Elias were still talking as they went through the back door of Paige's house.

"I was thinking," Elias said. "We'll get all the furniture in on Thursday, hook up appliances and finish up on Friday. How about getting married on Saturday morning?"

She swung around from putting her purse on the counter. "Saturday?"

"Yeah."

"Can you take off those days?"

"You bet. We're catching up with the hay and I'm taking some time off."

"Did you tell your mother about the wedding?"

Elias frowned. "No. Why?"

Maribel didn't know how to say what she was feeling so she was honest. "I'd like just the three of us at the ceremony—

you, me and Chase. I don't want a big deal made out of it. I'd rather it be private and just us."

"O-kay," he said slowly. "What about Grandpa? What about Rosie? What about my mom? They're going to feel hurt."

She rubbed a spot on the counter. "And that bothers you?"

"In a way. My mom's been at all my brothers' weddings and she's going to be hurt, especially based on what went on before."

Maribel threw up her hands. "Okay. I guess there's no way for us to get married in private."

"How about this?" Elias sat at the table. "I'll call Judge Henley and see if he can marry us at ten o'clock Saturday morning. Just us and no one else. And then I'll ask my mom if she could handle the reception at her house for the family."

Maribel thought about it and came to the conclusion that that was how it had to be. She took a deep breath. "I don't want to get married in the courthouse."

He sighed. "Where would you like to get married?"

"There's this gazebo in Horseshoe Park. It's white and has beautiful pink crepe myrtles blooming around it. I always thought it would be a beautiful place to get married."

Elias slapped his hand on the table. "The gazebo it is. At ten o'clock, and don't be late or I might marry someone else."

Maribel laughed. "I'm the only female in this county who will take you on."

He got up and slowly came toward her. She moved to the other side of the table and he advanced. Round and round they went until Chase came through the back door.

"What are y'all doing?"

"Arguing, son," Elias replied.

Chase shrugged. "Whatever cocks your pistol."

"That kid spends too much time with Grandpa."

Maribel clapped her hands. "And isn't it great? My city son is pure country now."

THE WEEK PASSED quickly. The furniture arrived on Thursday and they set everything up and the house looked so much better. Elias even spray washed the outside so even the exterior looked brand spanking new. On Friday, they cleaned Paige's house and mowed the yard. They planned to leave it just as they had found it. One more night and then they would be in their own home.

Maribel was nervous on Saturday morning as she slipped into that same white dress she'd bought on a whim. She was getting married. To Elias Rebel. At seventeen, that would've been a dream come true. Today, the passion and emotions of those two teenagers would be different. They were adults now and they would make adult decisions. But Maribel couldn't help but think the passion would be just as great.

Chase knocked on her door. "Mom, are you ready? It's time to go."

"Go with your dad. I'll be there in a few minutes."

"You're not backing out, are you Maribel?" Elias asked.

"No. I just don't want you to see me before the wedding."

"Ah, the romantic."

"I am not!"

She heard laughter on the other side of the door.

Sitting on the bed, she slipped into strappy white heels and stood to look at herself in the mirror. She had to look closely to see if it was her. She looked good. Her long hair hung down her back and she placed the floppy hat on her head. Just perfect for a wedding.

She drove to the park and sat for a moment, looking at Elias and Chase in the gazebo—both tall, dark and handsome. Anyone would know they were related because they looked so much alike. Her guys. Today, they would become a family.

Getting out of her car, she straightened her dress and walked up the steps to the gazebo. Judge Henley stood there with the Bible in his hand. Elias stared at her, as did Chase. What was wrong? Why didn't someone speak?

ALL ELIAS COULD do was stare. He knew Maribel was beautiful, but in her white dress she surpassed even his own dreams. Her long strawberry blonde hair was down her back just like he loved. He felt eighteen again and he knew now why he'd never got seriously involved with anyone else: he'd been waiting on Maribel.

"Wow, Mom. You look beautiful," Chase said and snapped a picture with his phone.

"Thank you, son."

Elias handed her a bouquet of miniature white roses.

"Oh." She seemed stunned. "I'd forgotten about the bouquet."

"You're gorgeous," he whispered in her ear, as he linked his arm through hers. And he knew they would be linked for the rest of their lives. The ceremony was over in a few minutes, and they were officially wed.

Judge Henley picked up his briefcase and pulled out some papers. He handed them to Chase. "Your father asked that your last name be changed and you signed the papers. You are now officially Chase McCray Rebel."

"Thank you, Judge."

"Just make sure you win the state championship this year."

"Yes, sir."

"And congratulations. I love happy endings."

As the judge walked off, Chase said, "We're officially a family."

With his arm around Maribel and the other around his son, Elias felt on top of the world.

THEY HEADED TO the ranch for the reception. Elias knew Maribel was nervous. But everything went off without a hitch. She fit into the family as if she were one of them, and she was now. Falcon and Quincy had barbecued and his mom had made all the trimmings with the help of the sisters-in-law. There was a tense moment when Ashton and Axel McCray showed up with their families. But his mom invited them in and Rosie, Remi and Maribel joined them. They started talking about kids and school and once again everyone did their best to get along.

Elias went to the kitchen where his mother was cutting another chocolate pie. "How many of those did you make?"

"I know you like chocolate pie so I wanted to have enough."

"I'm sorry if having the McCrays here bothers you."

She turned to look at him, her brown eyes sparkling. "I don't care who comes into this house as long as my son is back. I almost lost you. I don't want to live through that again." The sparkle turned to tears and he put his arms around her.

"I really love her, Mom."

"I know, as Paxton and Phoenix love their wives. That's just the way life is. You can't choose your kid's partners." She touched his face. "Never again do I want you to leave this ranch. Never."

"I won't," he reassured her. "My son is falling in love with the ranch and you'll probably see a lot of him."

"I couldn't think of anything I'd love more." She picked

up the pie. "Now let's see if anyone's hungry for more dessert."

Elias went to Maribel. She was laughing and talking and very animated. For a moment he just watched her. She was happy, but he had to wonder if she would ever love him the way he wanted her to. He would deal with that later, but for now he had what he wanted—a family.

MARIBEL WAS EXHAUSTED when they finally went home. She hadn't meant to stay that long, but visiting with her new family had just seemed right. She had been nervous at first, but Miss Kate had made everything perfect. She'd even made her brothers and their families feel welcome. That meant a lot to Maribel.

It was after eight o'clock when they walked through the back door of their very own house. She looked around at the new appliances, the furniture, the flooring, the walls and then at Elias. "Thank you. Everything is just what I wanted."

Elias threw his hat into the living room and it landed perfectly on the sofa. "Now comes the good part."

"Don't be crass." She walked toward the bedroom. "I don't see why Chase couldn't come home tonight. It's our first night in the house and he should be here."

Elias followed her. "He wanted to spend the night with Grandpa and I said yes. I didn't see any harm. He's getting to know his new family."

"But…"

"Let it go, Maribel."

She paused inside the doorway. She slowly laid her purse, bouquet and hat on the dresser beside a collection of white roses perched in the trash can that she had bought for Chase's room. Before she could ask questions, Elias walked in with a second trash can, the one she'd bought

for Grandpa's room, filled with ice and a bottle of champagne. In his other hand were two glasses.

"Why are you using trash cans?"

"I couldn't find a vase and we have no ice bucket. So trash cans it is." He placed everything on the dresser.

She shook her head and sat on the bed. "Sometimes you're so thoughtful and other times you're just crazy."

"And you love crazy." He sat beside her.

She took a deep breath. "I want to start this marriage being completely honest. You know how I feel about love. I just don't have those emotions in me anymore and if you're expecting it, maybe we should end this before it starts."

"Ah, Maribel, do you think I went to all this trouble if I didn't think there was a future for us?"

"Elias…"

"I've always been a gambler and I'm betting everything on you changing your mind. You can't keep everything inside. One day it's going to burst forth like a broken water pipe and you're going to realize that what happened with your mother is something you have to let go. Just like you have to let go of Chase and let him live his own life."

"I will never let go of my son."

"I didn't mean that. I mean you have to cut the apron strings." He sighed deeply. "And why are we talking about this?" He glanced at the flowers. "I just brought you some beautiful flowers and we should be celebrating."

"Why are they bent?"

"I had to shove them into the refrigerator and the trash can was kind of tall."

She laughed. She couldn't help herself. There was no one like Elias and maybe he was right. Maybe in the days ahead something in her would find a way to feel all the things he wanted her to.

She clasped her hands in her lap, needing to tell him something.

He removed his boots and set them neatly side by side. Looking at her serious face, he asked, "What now?"

She swallowed hard, trying to get the words out.

"Are you nervous?"

"A little."

"Come on. What's there to be nervous about? We've done this before." He stood and pulled his shirt out of his jeans.

"Well… You see…I…haven't…done it since Chase was conceived."

He stopped unbuttoning his shirt. "What? You mean…"

She nodded. "Yes. I mean I haven't been with anyone since that night."

"Are you kidding me?"

She glared at him.

He raised a hand. "Okay. You keep throwing these curveballs at me, Maribel. I thought we'd be butt naked and halfway to heaven by now."

"Don't be crass."

"Didn't you date in Dallas?"

"After a while, I did, but all the guys wanted was sex and I had a kid to think about. I didn't want an endless string of guys coming in and out of his life. I didn't want to have meaningless sex."

"Sometimes it's pretty good."

She glared at him again.

He walked over to the bottle of champagne and opened it. When the cork popped, she jumped. Her nerves were frayed and she just wanted him to understand how she was feeling. But with Elias, he probably only understood his point of view.

"I hope you don't think I'm sleeping in the other room tonight."

"No. I just wanted you to know."

He shoved a glass of champagne into her hands. "Drink up. It'll get rid of the nerves."

She took a sip of the refreshing bubbly. "Why aren't you nervous? Do men ever get nervous about sex?"

Elias laughed. "No. It's like breathing for men."

As she downed the rest of the bubbly, her face felt warm. Elias slipped out of his shirt and threw it on top of his boots. Then he poured more champagne. By the second glass, Maribel was wondering what she had been so nervous about, especially when he was kissing her all the way down her neck.

His hand gently slid down the zipper on her dress. She stood and shimmied out of it, standing in her fancy new bra and panties. She bent to remove her heels but Elias grabbed her and laid her on the bed. On his knees, he undid the straps of her heels and ran his hand up her leg. Her breath caught in an exquisite sigh and she wanted him to keep on touching her. He downed the last swallow of champagne left in his glass and took her empty glass from her hand, carefully setting them on the floor.

He looked into her eyes. "How are the nerves?"

"What nerves?"

He was out of his jeans and briefs in a heartbeat. Lying beside her, she reveled in his skin against hers. He slowly unhooked her bra and her panties went flying across the room. She heard a giggle and realized it had come from her. She never giggled. The champagne must be working. His lips touched her breasts and all thought left her as she gave into everything she'd been wanting.

She moaned as his lips found the most intimate part of her and he quickly brought them back to her breasts and

then to her mouth. The emotions and the passion were the same and nothing existed but the two of them in each other's arms, discovering all those special places known to lovers. His body was just as strong, hard and masculine as she'd remembered. Nothing had changed. The years had been kind to him. Her hands kneaded, stroked and teased until he groaned and slid on top of her.

They're joining was fierce and passionate with moans and sighs and Maribel held on to Elias and the spiraling pleasure until the last moment. They lay entwined, bathed in sweat, heart on heart. This was wonderful. This was part of being married.

She glanced at the slightly bent white roses on the dresser. Could her heart find a way to feel love again?

Chapter Fifteen

Elias never had a quitting time. He always worked until the job was done. But these days at five o'clock, like his brothers, he headed for the barn. He and Maribel had a small window of time that was theirs. It was before the kid came home from football practice and Grandpa showed up. It was the only time they had alone and they took advantage of it.

It was now October and Elias couldn't believe how fast time was flying. Hay season was over and they were back to ranching. He, Maribel and Chase had settled in to the house and it was as if they'd always been a family. Things were better than he'd ever expected. Maribel had been nervous that first night but now she was as insatiable as he was. Sometimes he'd even get a text from her in the early afternoon.

Are you coming home early?

That was when his workday ended and his nightlife began.

There were times in the throes of passion he wanted to say the words *I love you*. But he knew how she felt about the subject and he kept them to himself. He had to wonder, though, how much longer he could do that. He'd told

her that he didn't need her vows of love. He'd lied. Each day they grew closer and he hoped she was beginning to recognize that love wasn't a bad thing.

He rode into the barn on his horse, Budweiser, and Rico followed him. They'd spent the afternoon looking for a bull that had a knack for breaking fences. As he dismounted, his phone buzzed. He had a text from Maribel.

Can you come home early?

Rico took the reins of Elias's horse. "Go home. I'll take care of your horse."

"Thanks, Rico."

"That's what friends are for, and it's good to see you so happy."

Elias slapped him on the back. "Thanks, man."

He drove steadily home and then went through the back door, unbuttoning his shirt. He stopped for a moment and put on the safety chain. He didn't want any surprises from the kid or Grandpa. He threw his shirt into the laundry room and hopped out of his boots. In the doorway to the bedroom, he paused. Maribel was sitting on the bed, looking at something in her hand.

"You're still dressed."

"It's not always about sex, Elias."

"It is to me." He slipped out of his jeans.

"I wanted to talk about something."

"Later." He sat beside her and pulled her blouse over her head.

"Elias…" Her voice trailed away as his lips found her breast. A long time later, they lay on the bed entwined with the hum of their hearts beating together. They took a long, lazy shower and Elias rushed to get dressed.

"I have to pick up the kid in thirty minutes." He headed for the door and remembered she had wanted to talk. He turned and watched her shimmy into her tight jeans. That was something he never grew tired of. "You wanted to talk?"

She pulled her blouse on over her head. "Yes. But it can wait."

"No. I have a few minutes."

She picked up something from the floor that she'd dropped when he'd removed her blouse and then sat on the bed. "Gladys is thinking of selling the diner."

"Wow. It's been in her family for a long time."

"I know. She has two children and neither are interested in taking over. They don't even live here. Gladys is eighty-two and she wants to travel while she's still healthy."

"And this concerns us how?"

She looked straight at him and he could see a stubborn determination vivid in her eyes. "I want to buy it."

He eased down beside her. "We're kind of strapped for money since the house remodeling. But…"

She flipped back her long hair. "No, I want to do this on my own." She opened her hand and he saw a jewelry box. With one easy movement, she flipped the top and he stared at a gorgeous diamond wedding ring set.

"Where did you get those?"

"They're Miss Vennie's. She gave them to me and I tried to give them to her son after her death, but he wouldn't take them. He said I'd earned them for all the love and care I'd given his mother. I completely forgot about them when Chase was in trouble. But when I unpacked my stuff, I found them."

"They're beautiful rings."

She gently touched them. "And expensive. I told Miss Vennie they were too fancy for me and she said to put

them away for a rainy day when Chase and I needed something. She said they would be my security for the future. I thought about hocking them for an apartment in Dallas, but I couldn't do it then. Besides, it would have kept us in Dallas only for a little while and we still would've had to move."

"But you want to hock them now to buy the diner?"

"Yeah. I want something that's mine. Something I own so that a man can never take away my livelihood again. I felt so helpless back then."

And yet, she'd held on to the rings. They had some meaning to her and he hated to see her sell them.

"Ah, Maribel." He put his arm around her. "Keep the rings. We'll find a way to buy the diner."

She shook her head. "No. I want to do this. For me and for Miss Vennie. She would want me to."

"Are you sure?"

"Yes. I talked to Gladys and she wants to do the deal privately with a large down payment and then monthly payments for ten years. She's offering me a low interest rate. It's a good deal, Elias, and I can make the diner work even better. I can make the payments easily. I just need the down payment on the note." She looked at the rings. "And I'm hoping these rings will bring enough for me to do that."

"What about me and Chase? Are you going to have time for us?" Their life together was perfect to him and he was wondering if her business venture would interfere with that. And he felt a little jealous that she was taking steps away from him. But he could see how important it was to her and he wouldn't stand in her way.

She poked him in the chest. "I'll be the owner, silly. I managed a big restaurant in Dallas. I can do this, Elias, and I'd delegate much of the work. I plan to be home a lot." She scooted back, her eyes sparkling. "The whole diner

needs to be updated and painted inside and out. It needs new flooring and new ovens, even a pizza oven. And a big coffeemaker that will make lattes and an ice-cream machine for the kids. There are so many things that would make it a better place to dine."

Her enthusiasm got to him. "Okay. If it's what you want to do, I'm behind you all the way. I can do the flooring and the painting and putting in new appliances so you don't have to pay anyone."

She kissed his cheek. "You're so sweet. I don't know why people can't see that."

He laughed out loud and surprised himself. "Let's not tell anyone." He stood. "I'll take the rings to Temple to see what I can get for them."

"Thank you."

"I better go before the kid starts calling." Just then his phone buzzed and Elias looked at it. He showed the text to Maribel.

Grandpa came to practice and we're on our way home. Don't worry, Dad. I'm driving.

"Chase has been talking to Bubba about the red Silverado at his place. You know how Bubba is, he'll tell him to just to take it and try it out."

"Oh, no. That's not going to happen. I'll talk to Bubba."

"Zane has a truck and Chase wants one, too. I don't think he can wait till his birthday."

"He has to. It's just a few more weeks. He'll survive." Elias already had a truck picked out. The kid was getting it on his birthday. That was that.

He pointed to his head. "You see these gray hairs? They're all labeled *Chase*. We're making the barn into his man cave, as he calls it, so he'll have a place to hang

out with his friends. He's nesting, Maribel, and I think he just might like to stay in Horseshoe for the rest of his life."

"I wonder sometimes, too. He doesn't talk as much about football as he used to. But he still loves it. We'll have to wait and see how the year ends and let him make his own decisions."

Elias shook his head. "Oh, no. I'll have some say in his decisions. Sorry, that's just me. The kid wants to play football and he's going to give it his best shot. They've won every game so far and the future is looking good."

"Elias…"

"We'll talk to him after the season is over."

His phone buzzed again and he read the message and then held it out to Maribel.

Grandpa wants to pick up Mexican food so Mom doesn't have to cook. Yes or no?

Maribel took his phone and typed in Yes. "I want to go over some figures on my laptop for the diner and this will give me some time."

"Just remember the lights go out in here at ten o'clock."

She looked at him, mischief gleaming in her eyes. "Maybe, maybe not."

He walked out, thinking life was changing at too fast of a pace, but as long as his feisty Maribel was here at the end of the day, tough as nails, Elias could handle it.

Some days, Maribel had to pinch herself to believe some of the good things that were happening in her life. Elias got the price she wanted for the rings and the sale of the diner went through quickly. She chose colors, flooring and ordered appliances and Elias went to work. She painted the outside a fire-weed red with tan shutters and on the

inside one wall was the same color of red. They closed the diner on a Sunday afternoon and all day Monday, and she and Elias worked until it was finished. His brothers came in on Sunday afternoon to help move the heavy appliances and tile the bathrooms. It looked so much cleaner and fresher, especially with the new faucets. She didn't change the name. It was still The Horseshoe Diner. The booths needed to be re-covered, but that had to wait until she had more money.

The lattes were a big hit and every morning there was a line outside the door. She changed some items on the menu, but not a lot. For now, she was concentrating on making some money. And it was football season and the team was doing well. Tonight was homecoming and Chase was excited about that, and so was Elias.

A lot of people would be coming by the diner after the game. It would be a busy evening. She left the diner at four o'clock hoping to catch Elias before the game. As she opened her car door, she got a text from Elias.

Come home.

It wasn't the usual kind of text they sent each other. Something was wrong. She hurried through the back door to find Elias pacing in the kitchen.

"What happened?"

"Wyatt won't let Jody go to the dance with Chase."

"Why? I thought it was all set up. Zane and Erin and Chase and Jody were going together. Chase has talked about this for over a week."

"Wyatt found out. Evidently, Wyatt's wife didn't tell him Jody was going on a date with an almost eighteen-year-old boy. Jody called Chase crying and said she couldn't go. He's in his room, upset. Right before the game."

"Did you talk to Wyatt?"

Elias drove one fist into his hand. "No. If I go over there, I'll lose my temper."

Maribel laid her purse on the table, trying not to get angry, trying to see Wyatt's point of view. But all she could feel was her son's angst. He was a good kid and Wyatt knew that.

"I'll talk to Chase."

Elias caught her arm. "He's talking to Jody right now."

Before she could respond, Chase came into the room, smiling. Maribel's heart eased.

"After the game, we're going to meet at the dance. We're still going together, but I won't be picking her up. That's okay. I'll still be with Jody."

Elias put his arm around his son's shoulder. "Son, the sheriff is never going to accept you dating his daughter. He thinks you're too old for her."

"He thinks I'm like you, Dad, and that I'll get her pregnant."

At their son's words, Maribel could almost see the weight of the world on Elias's shoulders—his sins, his past mistakes.

"Everybody makes mistakes. That's what Grandpa says." Chase drew back to look at his father. "Do you see me as a mistake?"

"Not for one minute." Elias hugged his son.

"I don't want to be a father at eighteen," Chase said. "But someday I want to be a father just like you."

Elias hugged his son again and Maribel could see the words were now difficult for him. "Win that football game tonight."

"We will. And, Dad, can I take your truck?"

Elias handed him the keys.

"You know, Bubba still has that red Silverado."

"I know."

"My birthday's coming up."

"I know."

"Good." Chase smiled. "I don't want anyone to forget that."

"How could we?" Elias asked.

Maribel watched Elias with their son and marveled at their relationship in such a short period of time. They had connected and nothing could ever break their bond. There were times like these that she felt pressure in her chest as if something was pushing against the lock she had on her heart. The lock had grown weak, as if it was about to burst open with feelings she'd kept hidden for so long. She couldn't let that happen. The old fear was still there. They had something good and if she let go she was afraid it would all end.

FOOTBALL FEVER WAS taking over the town. The team kept winning and the town of Horseshoe was solidly behind them. Elias and Maribel made every game, even the ones out of town. The Rebel family didn't miss a home game, including his mom and grandpa. In the midst of everything, Chase's birthday finally arrived. It was on a school day and Elias's mom arrived early with a birthday cake. She'd insisted on making it and Maribel had let her. The whole Rebel family trickled in to celebrate the morning before Chase even woke up.

He bounced into the kitchen and stopped when he saw everyone and a big smile spread across his face as they all started to sing "Happy Birthday." They had cake and ice cream for breakfast and Chase opened gifts from the family.

Chase glanced at the clock. "We have to go to school, Zane. Can I take your truck, Dad?"

"No," Elias replied. "But you can take the one in the driveway."

Chase leaped to his feet. "You bought me the red Silverado?"

"No."

"Dad…"

Elias threw him a set of keys. "It may not be what you wanted, but…"

Chase ran for the door, not waiting to hear anything else. He stopped in the driveway as he stared at the new silver Silverado. He looked at Elias. "Is… Is this mine?"

"All yours," Grandpa answered. "Brand-new. No one's ever driven it, except Elias drove it home."

"Oh, man. Oh, man. Oh, man!"

"Aren't you going to try it out?" Elias asked. His son seemed in shock. Elias had searched and searched for the perfect truck, something he thought his teenage son would like. It had a lot of chrome and four-wheel drive.

Chase turned and hugged Elias. "Thank you!" And he turned to Maribel and hugged her. "I can't believe y'all bought me a new truck."

Zane opened the passenger side of the truck. "Are we going to school or not?"

Chase ran to the driver side and jumped in. He backed out and off to school they went. The family all left and Maribel and Elias stood in the driveway as if they couldn't move.

"I've never seen him so happy," Maribel said.

"Yeah," Elias agreed. But it was a tiny step Chase was taking away from them. Elias wanted to hold back time just for a little while to have his son at home. Like all fathers, though, he would change with the times and enjoy watching his son grow.

NOVEMBER WAS BUSIER than ever. The Horseshoe Cowboys kept winning. Elias and Maribel were on the road traveling from town to town to watch Chase play. Right before Thanksgiving, they won the playoffs and now would be playing for the state championship in the AT&T Stadium in Dallas. Chase was beside himself with joy and so was the family.

They had Thanksgiving at the ranch with the family. Elias watched as Maribel held Gracie, Rosie and Phoenix's daughter. She was so gentle and she'd probably been that way with Chase, too. That's why Chase had such a soft heart. He liked taking care of people, just as he'd taken care of his Nana. And now Grandpa. His boy was extra special and Elias had forgiven Maribel a long time ago for keeping him a secret.

DECEMBER ROLLED AROUND. The championship was on Thursday and the whole family was preparing to make the trip to Dallas. For the first time in a long time the ranch would be vacant. They didn't need to worry about the McCrays as they would be at the game, too. Gunnar's son, Dutch, was on the team and played defensive. Malachi's son, Dudley, was on the offensive line with Brandon Polansky. Chase had made friends with them both, but Zane still remained his best friend.

The night before they were to leave for Dallas, Maribel and Elias made love like it was their last time. It couldn't get much better. Her strawberry blonde hair was all around him and he cupped her face in his hands and said, "I love you, Mari." He couldn't hold it in any longer.

She stilled and pulled away from him. "No! Don't say that." She slipped from the bed and pulled on one of his old cotton T-shirts. "Why do you have to ruin everything?"

He pushed up against the headboard. "What are you talking about?"

"You said you didn't need vows of love."

"I lied. Every day I'm falling more and more in love with you, and if you'd just admit it, you'd realize that you feel the same way."

She shook her head. "No. Love just destroys everything."

"It doesn't, Maribel. Let's talk about your mother."

"No. I'm not talking about her."

"She said she loved you, but when it counted she didn't. That's the way you see it, right?"

"When my dad was beating me, she did nothing to help me. Nothing to help my baby. As I was leaving, she had the nerve to say, 'I love you, baby.' That's not love, Elias. I never want to feel that kind of love."

He looked at the sadness on her face and his stomach clenched as he saw all the hurt she was still wrestling with. He didn't know how to help her, but he knew she needed help.

"You feel love, Maribel. I know you do. Every time I see you looking at Chase, I see it. I see it when you're helping Grandpa with something. I see it even when you're laughing at me. I see it all the time in your eyes. All you have to do is admit it. Let it out, Maribel. Don't let Ira win this battle."

She pushed hair away from her face. "What?"

"If you keep all that pain inside you, you'll never be completely happy. And Ira wins. His cruelty wins. Don't let his cruelty destroy you. You have a wonderful son and you have me, loving you no matter what. Do something about it, Maribel, or you're going to lose everything."

He got up, slipped into his jeans and reached for his shirt. "If you don't, we have nothing. Without love, this marriage is nothing." He walked out the door.

Chapter Sixteen

Maribel sat on the floor and wrapped her arms around her legs. What had she done? Had she destroyed her marriage? She wanted to cry, but tears wouldn't come. Crying would mean she was weak and she wasn't. She knew she had a problem and she could handle it.

The sound of the truck had her jumping to her feet. She looked out the window and saw Elias's taillights pulling out of the driveway. Was he leaving her? *No!* She trembled from head to toe and admitted for the first time that she needed help. She couldn't lose her marriage. She couldn't lose Elias.

She hurriedly slipped on jeans and a blouse. Grabbing her purse, she ran for the garage. She knew where she was going. Mrs. Peabody was the only one she could talk to, but it was late and she might be asleep. She drove to her house and saw the lights were still on. Pulling out her phone, she searched for Mrs. Peabody's number and tapped it. In a few seconds, she was on the line and Maribel asked if she could come in for a minute.

Mrs. Peabody's white hair was in sponge rollers and so many memories of her childhood flashed through Maribel's mind. Her mother used to use those. Her mother...

"Come in, Maribel." Mrs. Peabody wrapped a flowered robe around herself.

"I know it's late and I don't mean to disturb you, but I really need to talk to someone."

"Have a seat. Would you like something to drink?" Mrs. Peabody's voice reminded her of Miss Vennie's. It had a soft undertone that drew people to them.

"No. Thanks. I'd just like to talk."

She sat on the tweed sofa. "You knew my mother better than anyone and I'd like to talk about her."

"Sarah was a sweet and timid soul and no one understood why she'd married Ira. Her parents were in their forties when she was born and as their only child they protected and sheltered her. I guess she was looking for adventure and excitement and hoping she could change a bad man. She found out quickly that wasn't possible."

Maribel told her about the beatings and the *I love you*s. "It's not love when you stand there and watch your child who is pregnant being beaten. After that, I don't feel love anymore."

"Oh, Maribel." Mrs. Peabody scooted closer and patted Maribel's leg. "Sarah loved you with all her heart and she loved you the best way she could. She was weak. She couldn't stand up to Ira. He beat her so much he broke her spirit. But she stayed because of her children."

"That's not love."

"When I saw her at the grocery store, she always asked about you and the baby. I showed her pictures you sent of Chase when he was born and I asked her if she would like to keep them. She said no. If Ira found them, he would kill her. And she had the twins and Rosie to think about. But every time I saw her, she wanted to see those pictures, Maribel. You may not understand that kind of love, but sometimes people love the only way they can."

A tear slipped from Maribel's eyes and she thought of all the years her mother had sacrificed to make sure they

had clothes and shoes to wear. She'd sold eggs and vegetables from her garden to make extra money and all of it had gone to her children. She'd stayed in an awful marriage because of them. Another tear slipped from her eyes and then another and then she was bawling like a baby.

Mrs. Peabody wrapped her arms around her. "Now, now, everything's going to be okay."

"She had a terrible life and I did nothing to make it better." She hiccupped and wiped away tears with the backs of her hands. "I was only thinking about myself. I never considered what she was going through."

"You made it better by just being in her life and she was so happy you found a good home. After Rosie got out of that disastrous marriage, she gave her money so she could rent an apartment and after she made sure Rosie was okay, she died quietly in her sleep. Her spirit couldn't take any more."

"Why didn't she ever call me?"

"When your parents were first married, Ira refused to let Sarah see her parents so she snuck off to visit with them. After Gunnar and Malachi were born, she would take them to visit. One day, Ira found out and he beat her to within an inch of her life. She stayed four days in the hospital and the sheriff at the time did nothing about it."

Maribel's eyes opened wide. She'd never heard that story. "And she went back?"

"She didn't want Ira to raise her babies and she was sure he would take them away from her. So, you see, she would never make that mistake again because of the twins and Rosie. She knew you were well and safe and being taken care of and away from Ira."

"I just…just…"

Mrs. Peabody pushed back Maribel's long hair. "Dry those tears and look at the life you have now. A wonderful

son, a good husband and you're a business owner. Don't let the past break your spirit. Don't let your father break your spirit like he broke your mother's."

Maribel drove home with her head spinning. So many years she'd had bad feelings toward her mother and now she wasn't sure what to feel, but she was clear on one thing: she was beginning to feel those deep emotions like she should. Her heart was opening up and love was there. She could almost touch it.

ELIAS HAD TO get out of the house or his temper was going to get the best of him. She was so stubborn. How could she not see how much he loved her? How could she not admit to everything they had? He'd given her time and time had run out for him. He wanted a full and complete marriage with a woman who loved him and he wanted her to say the words. It surprised him that he needed that. He'd always thought he wasn't like his brothers, but he was.

He went to Rowdy's for a beer. When he walked through the door, everyone shouted, "Elias!" and raised their beers. He nodded and sat at the bar.

Bob came over. "What are you doing in here? The honeymoon over?"

"Beer, please." He wasn't answering that question. It was nobody's business but his and Maribel's.

Bob placed a Bud Light in front of him. "Good to have you back."

"Yeah." Elias looked around at all the men and women drinking, talking, laughing and some dancing to the jukebox. This was his life before, but now he felt out of place. This wasn't his life anymore. He laid some bills on the bar. "See you later."

When he drove into the garage, he saw Maribel's car was gone. His heart took a nosedive. Had she left? Where

would she go at this time of night? And why? He walked into the house and it was dark and empty. And lonely. Without her, life had no meaning.

He sat down at the kitchen table and waited, glad Grandpa wasn't here tonight. He'd had supper with Paxton and his family and was coming early in the morning to go to Dallas with them. Chase was already in Dallas. Moonlight streamed through the windows and he didn't turn on the light. He couldn't stand the quiet. It was eating away at him. He pulled out his phone to call Phoenix, and then he heard her car. Unbelievable joy filled him and he knew he loved Maribel more than anything in this world. But how were they going to make this marriage work without love? Without her love?

She came into the kitchen, her hair all around her. "Where have you been?" he asked.

"Where have *you* been?" she countered.

"I went to Rowdy's for a beer."

She placed her purse on the table. "You didn't stay long."

"No. That's not my life anymore. Did you go to Rosie's?"

"I went to talk to Mrs. Peabody."

"Did it help?" He was hoping beyond everything that it had. At least she was trying and that meant a lot.

She pushed her hair away with a nervous hand. "I just need time, Elias. Please."

Oh, man. When she said *please*, he melted and realized he would do just about anything she wanted. "Okay."

"Okay," she said, and headed for the bedroom. After a moment, he slowly followed her and saw she was already curled up beneath the comforter. Usually, he would have wrapped his arms around her and they would have gone to sleep together. As much as he wanted to, he didn't reach out for her, though. He wasn't caving. He was seri-

ous about this. She had to come to grips with the past so she could live in the future. He just didn't know if he had that much patience.

MARIBEL COULD BARELY crawl out of bed the next morning. She'd been silently crying when Elias had come to bed. The relief she'd felt at his presence had only made her cry that much more, soaking her pillow with her tears in order to keep Elias from hearing her. She'd wanted to curl against him, but she resisted. Her mind was a mass of confusion.

After Elias was in bed, she'd thought back to the years of her childhood and had remembered all the times her mother had protected her from her father. She would make them turn down the TV and go to their rooms when she would hear his truck come home. She had never wanted them to get hit. Her mother could sew beautifully and she'd made a lot of Maribel's and Rosie's clothes. She had taught them how to sew and it was one of Maribel's fondest memories of time spent with her mother. So many things went through her mind and by the time she had finally fallen asleep, the resentment had ebbed away with the tears on her pillow.

She'd wanted to talk to Elias this morning, but there wasn't time. It would have to wait until after the game. Right now their focus was on Chase and the championship. She fixed breakfast, packed and then rushed to the diner to get things started for the day. Most people were headed for the game and there wouldn't be much traffic. Tomorrow, the diner would be closed as most businesses on the square would be, even the courthouse.

Grandpa was pacing in the breakfast room when she returned. She grabbed her bag, a couple of pillows and a blanket for Grandpa. It was a chilly December day and he'd probably go to sleep in the back seat.

Finally, they were on their way. Grandpa talked most of the time, but as expected, he was soon snoring. Elias didn't say anything, just drove steadily toward Dallas. She didn't feel like talking, either. She was tired. She pushed back the seat and thought about Christmas. They still had to get a tree and she had to go shopping. The easy movement of the truck lulled her into a relaxed state. In her mind, one word kept humming: *tomorrow, tomorrow*. She and Elias would talk and hopefully she could open up and say exactly what she was feeling. Tomorrow.

IT WAS LATE afternoon by the time they got to Dallas and checked in to their rooms. They all went over to the hotel where the football players were staying and visited with Chase. He was nervous about tomorrow, but then they all were.

The next morning, they were up early, had breakfast and headed for AT&T Stadium. They found their seats and soon the whole Rebel family arrived. Grandpa sat by him and his mother sat by Maribel. The rest of the family sat around them. Wyatt and Hardy and their families, including Bubba's family, the Wiznowskis, were to their right. Judge Henley's family and friends were to the left. The McCray clan gathered behind them. The town of Horseshoe was well-represented. Just about everyone was there.

Since Horseshoe was a small school, the game started at 11:00 a.m. The bigger schools' championship games were later in the day. Chase waved to them from the field, but now his focus was on football. The Cowboys were in blue and white. The Oakridge Cougars were on the other side of the field in red and white. They hadn't lost a game, either and that worried Elias. They were going to be a tough team to beat.

The Cougars won the toss and elected to receive. The

first half was a nail-biter. By the time it ended they were tied at 14–14. The Cougars were shutting down Billy Tom and he was having a rough time getting the ball off to Chase. Plus, he was getting banged-up. The second half was just as tense. The Cougars scored in the third quarter and they were up by seven. The Horseshoe Cowboys were struggling and Elias felt like he had acid in his stomach. Then Billy Tom got away and lobbed a pass to Chase and they tied it up. But the Cowboys were getting tired and the Cougars still looked fresh. They were down at the ten-yard line ready to score again, but the Cowboys held them to a field goal. The score was 24–21 and time was running out. With six seconds left on the clock, they had the ball on the fifty-yard line. Coach Pringle called a timeout.

"Chase is going to be devastated if they lose," Maribel said.

"It's not over yet," Grandpa replied. Elias was too nervous to speak. The Cougars on the sidelines were already celebrating. They were holding up signs that read State Champs.

"What can they do?" Maribel asked. "They're too far away for a field goal to tie it and they keep sacking Billy Tom."

"They have to get the ball to Chase. That's what they have to do," Grandpa told her.

The guys were in a circle on one knee and Coach Pringle was in the center with a clipboard and paper. He was drawing plays and the guys were listening. They needed a miracle.

"It has to be a Hail Mary pass to Chase." Elias finally found his voice. "That's the only way they can win this thing."

Nobody responded because they all knew the team had

been trying to do that most of the fourth quarter and had been unsuccessful. They had Chase covered like a blanket.

The teams lined up again for the last six seconds. Everyone was on their feet and holding their breaths. The center hiked the ball to Billy Tom and the Cougar defense was fast on him. He quickly tossed the ball to the running back, Pee Wee Polansky, Brandon's younger brother. Pee Wee drew back and threw the ball as hard as he could toward the end zone and Chase. Everyone watched as it spiraled, spiraled and spiraled toward Chase. Three Cougar players surrounded him.

Elias watched with his heart in his throat. "It's over his head," Elias shouted. "Dammit."

Maribel grabbed his hand and squeezed. He held on as the ball came down over Chase's head. But with his right hand, he reached back and tipped it forward. It bobbled in the air and everyone leaped for it. Chase's hands were there first and he brought it down to his chest and fell to the ground.

The referee signaled touchdown. The clock ticked to zero. The Horseshoe Cowboys had won in a last-minute thriller. Pandemonium ensued. The team piled on Chase, but he wiggled out and ran toward Elias and Maribel. He climbed over people, benches and into the stadium. He grabbed Maribel and Elias and hugged them.

"We did it, Dad! We did it. Did you see?"

"You bet I did." He hugged his son so tight his arms hurt.

"This is for you, Dad." He handed Elias the football. "I'll sign it when we get home."

His throat closed up and words eluded him as he took the football.

"Do you think the scouts were watching?" Chase asked.

"You know they were," Grandpa replied, holding on to

Chase with all his strength. Scouts were already recruiting him. They'd gotten several calls and offers. Chase was going to play college football. He just had to make up his mind where he wanted to go. People were shaking his hand and patting him on the back. Elias noticed Coach Pringle trying to get their attention.

"Coach wants you back on the field," he said to Chase. "And you ran right by Jody. She was waiting for you."

"Oh, man. Oh, man. I gotta go." He leaped from the stands back onto the field and ran straight toward Jody, grabbing her and swinging her around in a bear hug.

Elias looked toward Wyatt and he was frowning. *Get used to it, Wyatt.*

He was finally able to relax as he watched his son being interviewed on television. It was a day Elias would never forget. They stayed and watched all the festivities. Chase received the Most Valuable Player award and the team raised the championship trophy high with smiles on their faces. Zane was snapping pictures like crazy, as was Maribel. There would be a lot of pictures and reminders of this day for a lifetime.

THEY ARRIVED BACK in Horseshoe at around eight o'clock that night and Maribel was exhausted from all the excitement. People had already put signs along the highway: State Champs. It was the first state championship for this small town and everyone was elated.

She got a call from the principal's secretary. The kids were getting the day off tomorrow from school. They had to show up for their first class and check in and then the town was throwing the football players a big party in the gym. She'd asked if Maribel could bring food and Maribel had agreed. The whole town was excited.

A honking of a horn alerted them that Chase was home.

Elias ran for the back door and Chase came through it, smiling. More hugs and smiles. And then Chase talked on and on about the trick play.

"How did you catch that thing?" Grandpa asked.

"I don't know," Chase admitted. "I saw the ball in my peripheral vision and I just tried to reach it. When I touched it, I tried to bring it down, and I don't know, I managed to get it in my hands."

And on and on it went, and then the phone calls started. Everyone in the family wanted to congratulate Chase. It was midnight before they even thought about going to bed.

"Hey, Mom, there's a big party at school tomorrow."

"I know. I'm bringing food."

"We'll be out the rest of the day." He turned to Elias. "Can I have a party in my man cave tomorrow with all my friends?"

"Yes. But no beer," Elias replied.

Chase gave him a thumbs-up sign. "Deal."

Maribel went to bed completely drained, but in a good way. Elias slipped in beside her, but they didn't touch and that bothered her. She had to do something because it was all on her. She was too tired to think too much, but tomorrow she would have to address the real problem in her life.

The next morning, she was up early to go to the diner to make hero subs to take to the gym. Chase had already left for school and Grandpa had gone home to feed his dog.

Elias came into the kitchen for coffee.

"I'm going to the diner to make food for the party. I'll be there as soon as I get everything started at the diner. There won't be much business until the party is over."

Elias leaned against the counter, sipping his coffee. "Tonight we're going to talk and neither one of us is coming out of the bedroom until you say the words I want to hear."

"Have you forgotten? We'll have about thirty kids here tonight. We have to chaperone."

"I told Chase the party ends at ten o'clock and that's when we'll talk." He placed his cup in the sink and walked out.

Chapter Seventeen

Elias had decided he had to do something about his marriage. He wasn't the type of person to let things go. He was a doer and he had to make a big decision about their relationship. The status quo wasn't working. She had to open up and feel everything he was. At the game when she'd reached for his hand, he'd known she had feelings for him. She just had to admit it.

On the way to the school, he stopped by Wyatt's office. He wanted to talk about Chase and Jody.

Wyatt was sitting at his desk, writing in a file. He looked up. "Hey, Elias. That was some game, wasn't it?"

Elias eased into a chair. "Yep. Chase's feet still haven't touched the ground. It'll probably take a couple weeks. He's having a party later this afternoon, and I hope you'll let Jody come. Maribel and I will be there to watch over things."

Wyatt leaned back in his chair. "She's sixteen and he's eighteen. Up until he arrived in Horseshoe, her only concern was her grades and college and now he's all she talks about. She's too young to get involved with anyone. She doesn't even date. I'm not happy about this situation."

"I don't want Chase to get serious about someone either, but I think it's out of our control."

"No, it isn't. She's sixteen and she'll do what I tell her

and she's not getting involved with an eighteen-year-old boy."

Elias laughed. "Oh, Wyatt. Of the two of us, I always thought you were the smarter one. If you refuse to let her see Chase, she'll sneak out and see him. The attraction is not all on Chase's side. Would you rather she does that or would you rather monitor what she's doing? I'd rather know where Chase is than have him sneaking around."

Wyatt ran his hand through his hair. "Seems like yesterday she was running in here with her dog, Dolittle, wanting me to go fishing and then getting mad because I had to work. She grew up too fast."

"Mine grew up without me in his life. Let me tell you, that's not a good feeling."

Wyatt pointed a finger at Elias. "I'll let her come, but you better watch them."

"Like a duck on a June bug."

Wyatt smiled.

"Sheriff!" Stewart shouted from his desk. "Freddie Kuntz just called. He says he's at the school and he's planted bombs. I don't know if it's a hoax or not but he says you better get there in a hurry."

Wyatt was on his feet in an instant and reached for his hat. "That kid is nothing but trouble. He, his brother and his cousin got expelled from school two weeks ago for smoking marijuana and doing PCP. They spent a few days in jail and the cousin's mother got them out. Their trial is coming up in two weeks and they'll probably spend some time in juvie or even prison."

Elias hadn't seen Freddie in a while. He'd been too busy with football, but he hated to hear the boy was on drugs. He followed Wyatt to the school. Cars were parked everywhere and there was an eerie quiet around the school. No one was going in or coming out. Wyatt got out of his

car with a megaphone. They could see Freddie standing inside behind the glass doors with the school microphone in his hand. He wore fatigues and a red bandanna around his head.

"Hey, sheriff, how you doing? Scooter, Leonard and I are doing just fine. We're not going to prison and you know why?"

"What are you up to, Freddie?"

"Well, you see, sheriff. The principal expelled us from school and we couldn't go to the football game. So we decided to get even. There's a bomb on every outside door and window of the school. While everyone was celebrating, we were hard at work."

"You don't know how to make a bomb, Freddie."

"Okay, sheriff. The first bomb is going to go off in exactly fifty-two seconds. It's the principal's office. He gets it first for expelling us."

"Is he for real?" Elias asked.

"Let's hope he's joking. That kid's not smart enough to make a bomb."

Elias looked at his phone. "If he's not, the bomb should go off right about now." As the words left Elias's mouth, they heard the explosion and smoke spewed up from where the principal's office was located.

"Hot damn, sheriff. What do you think now?"

"Holy crap." Wyatt was on the phone with local law enforcement and the FBI. Freddie wasn't joking. This was serious. Wyatt called in all the volunteer deputies. They checked the principal's office and couldn't get in or see anything. Beams obstructed the window.

"What do you want, Freddie?" Wyatt asked. "You must want something."

"You're darn right, I do. We have everybody locked in the gym. Just about everybody in this town is sitting on

the floor. Some are crying, some are begging, wanting their mamas. They're a joke."

"Jody's in there," Wyatt said under his breath.

"Chase is in there," Elias added.

People started to gather around and Wyatt gave Stewart orders to hold everybody back. Hardy arrived and so did Judge Henley. Rico walked up to Elias.

"What are you doing here?" Elias asked.

"I was picking up feed and someone said there was a bomb at the school so I came to check it out. Most of the family is in there."

"What?"

"The women came in to help with the party, except Paige. She had to go to work. But everyone else is in there with some of the kids."

"Is my mother in there?"

"No. She and Grandpa were coming later."

"Oh, man." Elias had heard this happening in other towns, but not here in safe Horseshoe, Texas. It couldn't be happening.

Peyton, Wyatt's wife, and Angie, Hardy's wife, ran to Wyatt. "Our kids are in there," Peyton told Wyatt. "I let J.W. go with Jody. He didn't want to miss anything. And Angie let Trey go with Erin. Our kids are in there, Wyatt. Do something."

Elias could see Wyatt was trying to maintain his composure. "Peyton, law enforcement will deal with this."

"Wyatt…"

People gathered around on their phones, trying to reach the people inside to no avail. Wyatt was also on his phone. He clicked off. "A SWAT team from Temple is on the way. It'll take fifteen to twenty minutes. The FBI said to stand down until they get here."

"Are you listening, sheriff?" Freddie bellowed through

the microphone. "Here's what we want. We want a hundred thousand dollars in cash, no large bills, and a brand-new pickup truck. If we don't get it, this place is going to go up like it's the Fourth of July. The first bomb has already gone off and in one hour another one will go off and then one will go off every five minutes. Do you want to test me on that one, sheriff? We're ready to die. Are you ready to watch your kids die?"

"Okay, Freddie. I'll need more than an hour."

"You have an hour, sheriff. That's it. And if anyone comes near a window or a door, I'll trigger the bombs to go off and you can say goodbye to most of the people in this town."

"Freddie, I need more time."

Freddie disappeared from the front of the school and in a moment they heard him again on the microphone. "Sheriff, I'm standing in front of your daughter and she's holding your son. She sure is a pretty thing. I can kiss her and you can't do anything about it."

Wyatt tensed.

"And, Mr. DA, your daughter is right here, too. A pretty blonde holding a little boy who's glaring at me. I bet I can make them cry. What do you think?"

"Leave them alone." That was Chase's voice and Elias clenched his fist.

"I'm fixing to put the butt of this AK-47 in Chase Rebel's face. Let's see how tough the big football hero is."

"Come on, Freddie. Don't hurt my son," Elias grabbed the megaphone from Wyatt.

"Elias? Is that you?"

"Yeah, Freddie, it's me."

"Tell the sheriff I'm serious."

"He knows and he's working on getting the money.

If it's not enough time to get a truck here, you can have mine."

"Hot damn! Now we're talking. You got any beer, Elias?"

Elias looked at Wyatt and whispered, "Get some beer." Two six-packs were shoved into his hands.

"Yeah. I got beer."

"Bring it in. I'll let you in the side door, but no one else. If I sense anything funny, I'll pull the trigger on these bombs. Understand?"

"Sure thing. I'm on my way."

"The FBI said stand down, Elias. We don't know what's going on in there."

"We have about fifty-five minutes to get those people out of there. If he's willing to let me in, I'm going in to try to talk him down. I'm not waiting around for the FBI. My son is in there and I'll never stand down. Never."

Wyatt threw up his hands but didn't say anything. Elias walked toward the side door and no one tried to stop him. Rico fell into step beside him.

"What's your plan?"

"Go back to the group, Rico. If Freddie sees you, it could be dangerous."

"You need backup."

There were three guys inside with AK-47s. Elias didn't know what was waiting for him. He didn't want to endanger Rico's life, but he would need help.

He stopped to face Rico. "Okay. When he opens the door, I'll try to distract him and you put your fingers in the door jamb so it doesn't close completely. If it closes, we're out of luck and I'll have to handle him alone. Just be careful and make sure that he doesn't see you."

"Got it. I can be as quiet as a mouse."

Elias looked back at Wyatt who was watching him

closely, but he didn't call him back. Wyatt's kids were in there, too.

He tapped on the door and he heard scrapings on the other side. In a minute, it opened a crack and Freddie's glazed eyes looked around. "You alone?"

Elias held up the two six-packs. "Just me and the beer." Rico was standing flat against the building so Freddie couldn't see him.

Freddie opened the door a little wider and Elias slipped in. He stepped in front of Freddie, forcing Freddie to face him with his back to the door. He pulled a beer from a six-pack and held it out. "Have a beer, Freddie. It'll calm you down."

The boy's eyes were glassy and Elias knew he was on something. He tried not to look at the door so as not to draw Freddie's attention to it. He stepped back farther and Freddie took a step toward him to get the beer. The rifle was still in his hand with his finger on the trigger. He took the beer with his other hand.

"You're a good man," Freddie said.

Rico crawled in like a snake and slithered down the hallway. Freddie turned around quickly. "Did you see something?"

"No. It's just us."

Freddie swung toward the door. "I have to set this or those dumb cops will come rushing in." Elias watched as Freddie did something with his phone. All the while, Freddie kept one eye on him.

"What are you doing?"

"Resetting the bomb above the door. I bet you didn't think I was that smart, did you, Elias?"

Elias shook his head. "Did you make these bombs?" There was something like a can with wires hanging down

attached above the door. Elias had never seen anything like it in his life.

"Yep. Scooter sorted it all out. We got it off the internet. We didn't understand it all so we made some adjustments. Everybody thinks Scooter's dumb, but he isn't. He figured out how to hook up all these bombs to my mom's phone and all I have to do is push a button and the school goes up like a big ol' dark cloud."

So that meant no one could get out or come in. The bombs were set.

"What are you doing, Freddie? These kids haven't done anything to you."

Freddie laughed. "They've bullied me, my brother and my cousin all our lives. It's payback time, Elias. Once we get the money and the truck, we'll be gone."

"How are you going to get out of here?"

Freddie held up his phone. "I can turn this door bomb off with my phone and turn it on again as we leave. Once we're out of sight, I can turn it off again. Genius, isn't it?"

Elias nodded his head. "Yeah, Freddie. I'm impressed. Just don't understand why you want to do this."

"The principal said we couldn't come back to school because we smoked some weed in the bathroom. Everybody smokes weed. And the DA and the sheriff said they were going to put us in prison. We're not going to prison."

"Freddie…" Elias took a step toward the boy and Freddie pointed the gun at him.

"You're asking a lot of questions."

Elias held up his hands. "You wanted some beer and I brought it just like all the times I saw you walking and gave you a ride. I'm just trying to help."

Freddie waved the gun around. "Do you know how many rounds I can shoot with this thing?"

"More than I want to know," Elias replied. "Where did

you get something like that?" The kid never had any money and Elias didn't know how he got the money to set this up.

"My mom's boyfriend works in a gun shop in Temple. When we got expelled, my mom told him to take us with him because we were driving her crazy. We wanted to go to the movies, but he wouldn't give us any money. So we sat around the gun shop all day and when he was with a customer, we snuck the guns out and hid them in the truck. Later, we hid them in the backyard. If we were going to take out the people of Horseshoe who had hurt us, we were going to need firepower." Freddie laughed, a chilling sound. "The jerk got arrested when the owner found the guns missing, and he's in jail."

Elias needed to take Freddie down here so he could deal with the other two later, but he wasn't getting an opening. The gun was pointed at his chest and Rico wasn't going to pounce until Freddie moved the gun. He didn't. Instead, he waved with the beer can. "Go to the gym. Scooter wants a beer."

Elias had no choice but to walk toward the opening that lead to the gymnasium. He paused in the doorway. The gym was packed with students, teachers and parents getting ready for the party and he saw fear in their eyes. His sisters-in-law sat together and he saw Jake, John, Annie, Martha Kate and Justin. Man, the kids were here with their mothers. Cell phones were on a pile in one corner. There were two tables of food and it looked as if Freddie and his friends had already helped themselves.

Chase sat in the front with Zane, Erin and Jody. He jumped to his feet when he saw Elias. Scooter pointed the gun at him and shouted, "Down."

Chase eased back to the floor.

"If anybody else jumps up, you're dead meat. I'm tired of dealing with you," Freddie yelled.

"Yeah," Scooter mumbled angrily. He was mad and hyped up on something. He was big and stout and it would be hard to take him down. Elias searched for a way to get everybody out of there safely. He didn't know if he could do it, but he was grateful Maribel wasn't here.

MARIBEL WOKE UP to searing pain. She couldn't understand what was wrong. Her whole body ached and her head throbbed. She reached up to touch her head and it felt wet. Looking at her hand, she saw it was blood. *Blood!* She realized some other things, too. She was lying on the floor with something. Dust filled her nostrils and stuff was pressing up against her body. Where was she? Was she dreaming?

She coughed and tried to sit up. More dust and debris rained down on her head and she suddenly remembered where she was. She'd brought the sandwiches to the school and Chase had helped her take them in. When they were walking out, they had met Cindy and Cheryl, Gunnar's and Malachi's wives, with their two little girls. They had brought food and were running late. They had to take Amber and Kelly to the principal's office to get a tardy slip so they could go to class and to the party. Maribel had offered to take the girls to the principal's office so Cindy and Cheryl could continue to carry the food inside.

Once they were there, they could hear someone talking on the school microphone. Something about bombs. Principal Gaston had tried the door and had found it was locked. He'd pulled out his phone to call the sheriff and all Maribel remembered was a loud sound. Had it been a bomb?

She wiped dust from her face and looked around. There was debris and rubble everywhere. A steel beam lay across the single window and another beam was across where the door used to be and electrical wires were hanging down,

giving off sparks. Principal Gaston lay on top of his flattened desk. Oh, no!

She crawled through the rubble to where he lay. Blood oozed from his head and she didn't know if he was alive. She searched for a pulse and found one. It was faint, but it was there. She found a handkerchief in his coat pocket and pressed it against the cut on his head to stop the bleeding.

Then it hit her. Where were the girls? She looked around and saw they were trapped under a steel beam. She crawled over to them. They were both knocked out but alive. Their legs were under the beam. Maribel tried to move it, but she wasn't strong enough. Her efforts only caused more debris to fall. She sat between them and wiped dust from their faces.

Where was everyone? Why wasn't someone coming to help them? Principal Gaston needed medical attention. "Help!" she screamed over and over. There was no answer but eerie silence. She grew dizzy and crawled into a ball to stop it. And then she prayed.

Sometime later, she heard a voice and she opened her eyes, however, she didn't see anything but the devastation around her. No one had come to help them.

I love you, Maribel.

She heard the voice clearly and she pushed into a sitting position. There was a presence in the room and she could feel it. It was her mother. Was Maribel hallucinating? The dizziness intensified, but the voice was clear and riveting. *I love you, Maribel.*

All the resentment through the years of hating her mother seemed trivial compared to what she was trapped in now. She'd been like an angry little girl throwing a temper tantrum because her mother didn't love her the way she wanted. But she'd loved her the only way she could. Everything was so clear now.

I love you, Maribel.

"I love you, Mama," she responded, and the presence was gone. "No, come back. I need you." Feeling drained, she lay back on the floor.

Her heart was lighter and hope burned in her chest. Elias would get them out of here, she was sure. All she had to do was wait for him.

And the words she couldn't say came easy. "I love you, Elias." Would she ever get to say them to him?

Chapter Eighteen

"Everybody stay calm," Elias said to the group.

"Y'all better listen to him," Freddie said. "My trigger finger's getting antsy."

Elias stepped to one side while Scooter and Freddie guzzled down the beer. Leonard was standing on two desks at the back with his gun pointed toward the group. Damn! He couldn't jump Freddie and Scooter without Leonard shooting everyone.

"Hey, Leonard!" Freddie shouted. "Come get some beer. No one's going to move. They're scared to death."

Leonard jumped off the desk and made his way to the front. The three boys were in the middle drinking beer and Elias was on the outside. He saw Rico outside the doorway. He could jump them now and Rico would help. But the guns bothered Elias. They could start shooting and someone could get hurt. Was he willing to take that risk?

Suddenly, Freddie pointed the gun at Elias. "Call the sheriff. Ask him where's our money. If we don't get it in five minutes, we're going to start shooting people like sitting ducks. Got it?"

Getting drunk on drugs was not a good thing. Elias could see Freddie was losing it. "Okay, just stay calm."

"Put it on speakerphone so I can hear everything."

Elias did as Freddie asked and Wyatt answered the

phone. "Freddie wants to know where the money is. I'm in the gym and everybody is here. He needs the money now or he's going to start shooting people. Do you understand, Wyatt?" *Get the damn money*, he said in his head.

"The money is here," Wyatt replied.

"How about the truck?" Freddie asked.

"Yes, it's here, too."

"Hot damn. Now we're talking!" Freddie shouted. "Bring the truck to the parking lot outside the side door. Leave the motor on and the doors open. Put the money in the back seat. And, sheriff, don't try anything funny. The bombs are still set to go in about forty-two minutes. If you shoot me, everyone in here is dead because I'll reset it as soon as I walk out the door. I'll turn it off when we're safely away. Understand?"

"I understand, Freddie, but what guarantee do I have that you'll turn off the bombs?"

"You don't. You have to trust me. Isn't that a kick in the head? But you see, I'm fond of Elias and I wouldn't kill him because he's the only person in this town who's ever helped us."

"I'm trusting you, Freddie."

"Let's go," Freddie said to Scooter and Leonard. "We got what we wanted." He turned to the group. "Everybody better stay seated if they want to live."

"They will," Elias said. "I'll make sure of that."

The boys backed out of the gym with the guns pointed at them. At the door, Freddie said, "So long, Elias." Then running footsteps echoed loudly in the hallway.

"Everybody stay down!" Elias shouted, and then he said to Rico as he followed the boys, "Make sure they all stay down." Elias ran as fast as he could, hoping to catch the side door before it closed. If he could, then Freddie couldn't reset the bombs. The boys were at the door and Elias was

almost there. Freddie didn't look back. They ran through it and Elias made a dive for the door, but not in time. He heard the click. Freddie had reset it.

"Dammit. Dammit. Dammit!" His phone buzzed.

"Is everyone okay?" Wyatt asked.

"Yes. What's happening?"

"They're getting in the truck and now they're driving away."

"Keep everyone away from the school, Wyatt. Freddie reset the bombs and we're trapped in here until he deactivates it."

"Are you sure about the bombs? They could be fooling us."

"I've seen one on the side door and some on a few windows so I'm guessing they're on every door and window like he said. Whether they go off or not, I'm not sure, but I'm not willing to take that chance. Are you?"

"The bomb squad is here. Take several pictures of the bombs and send them to me. The FBI will be taking over."

"The bombs are going to go off in forty-one minutes, Wyatt. We don't have time for cops to jockey for position here."

"Oh, no!" He heard Wyatt cursing.

"What happened?"

"The FBI put spikes on Highway 77 and stopped the truck. There was a shootout and the boys are dead."

"Dammit, Wyatt! The bombs are still set! Didn't the FBI realize that?"

"Like I said. They're taking over now."

"Get Freddie's phone as fast as you can. You can turn off the bombs with it. Surely some of those geniuses can figure it out."

After a moment Wyatt came back on the line. "Fred-

die's phone is in a hundred pieces. They're getting someone to look at it."

"We don't have that much time." Elias took a deep breath and it burned his lungs. He was dealing with a bunch of idiots. Everyone in here was going to die unless he got them out.

He quickly took photos of some of the bombs and sent them to Wyatt.

"What's happening?" Rico asked.

Elias turned to his friend. "We're trapped in here. The FBI just killed the boys on Highway 77 and Freddie didn't deactivate the bombs. I have to figure out a way for us to get out of here. Just try to keep everyone calm in the gym."

"Chase and Jody are taking care of that. They have everyone reciting Bible verses."

"Good. Let's see if bombs are on every outside window and door." Elias ran down the hallways, looking for bombs, as did Rico. They met back at the side door. "What did you find?"

"Every window and every door that leads outside has that strange contraption on the top of it," Rico replied.

"They weren't bluffing. But maybe they weren't smart enough to ensure that every bomb went off every five minutes after an hour. We can only hope." He paced back and forth. "I can't just wait for that. I have to do something. There are so many lives involved."

He called Wyatt. "Has the bomb squad come up with anything?"

"They're looking at it now. They say it needs a code."

"I know that. Freddie had the code on his phone."

"They're working on it."

"Once again, Wyatt, we don't have time for them to look things up. Someone has to figure this out. Now!"

"The bomb squad wants to come in."

"How? I just checked and there are bombs on every door and every window. If they activate one, they all go off. That's what Freddie said and I believe him. Are they willing to kill everybody in here?"

"The FBI has arrived and they're taking over."

"Like hell. You better answer your phone when I call. I'm looking for a way out. Tell them to stay away until then."

"There's no other way out of here, Elias," Rico reminded him.

Elias paced again. "I went to school here and I'm thinking of all the ways I snuck in when I was late." Suddenly, he remembered something Maribel had said. He snapped his fingers. "I got it." He ran down the hall to the janitor's closet. Rico followed him.

There wasn't a bomb on the door because it was just a big closet with cleaning supplies.

"There's nothing in here," Rico said.

Elias pointed to another door. "There's a stairwell that leads to the roof. When I was a teenager, Bubba and I brought beer to school and got drunk. We were drinking in here and discovered the stairwell. I went up it and jumped off the roof as a superhero. Today, that teenage foolishness is going to pay off. Let's pray there's no bomb at the top of the stairs." Elias flipped on the light and saw nothing at the top. Freddie didn't know about the stairs. "It's clear. This is a way out."

He ran back to the gym. "Everyone, listen to me carefully. In a second I want you to quietly line up, single file, without pushing or shoving. Those who have a handicap will come first and please come forward because I don't want to have to deal with that later. It will only slow us down and we only have thirty-nine minutes. Mrs. Edgars, I know you have arthritis so you will go first, and then Mr.

Weatherby, because I know you have a heart condition. Mrs. Lopez, you have a pacemaker so you will go next." Elias waited for Remi to say she needed help, but he knew she wouldn't. She'd been in a serious accident and had a bad leg as a result of it. He didn't know if she could make it up the narrow stairs, so he was going to have to force it. "Remi, you will go next."

"Elias…"

He held up his hand. "No arguing. I don't have time and neither do you. Line up and Rico will lead you out. Just follow orders, that's all I'm asking." Elias hurried out to the janitor's closet and went up the stairs. He pushed open the door and stepped out on to the roof. Then he pulled out his phone and called Wyatt.

"I'm on the roof. I need two tall ladders right here where I'm standing. It's about eight feet where there are no bombs. We can't go any farther than that."

"What the…?"

"I don't have time to explain. Just get the ladders so we can get everyone out of here."

"We can use a fire truck."

"No," Elias replied. "It too risky getting a big truck that close. Just get the ladders."

"Are you ready?" Rico shouted to Elias.

He saw guys with ladders running toward the school. Once they were in place he shouted back to Rico. "Start bringing them up. I'll help on this end. We have to go fast."

The elderly teachers came first and firefighters came up the ladders to help them down. When Paxton saw Remi with Annie, he shot up the ladder before anyone could stop him. He grabbed Remi, who was holding Annie, and carried them down the ladder. "Thank you, Elias."

The students, teachers and family members kept coming. Elias rushed them to the ladders and down to safety.

All the time, he kept looking at his phone. Time was ticking away. But everyone was cooperating and going as fast as they could. That helped. They all wanted to get to safety. The football players came last and then there was just Chase, Rico and Elias.

"Go," Elias said to his son.

Elias's phone buzzed. "Two of the McCray kids didn't come out," Wyatt said. "Gunnar's and Malachi's daughters, Amber and Kelly. They're five years old."

"Are you sure? There's no one else in there."

"They're in there somewhere, Elias."

"I'll have to go back in." He had three minutes before the next bomb went off. Damn!

"Oh, no." Chase ran his hands over his face.

"What's wrong?" Elias asked. "And what are you still doing up here?"

"Mom…"

"What about Mom?"

"She… She…"

Elias had a foreboding feeling in his stomach. "What is it, Chase?"

"I think Mom is in the principal's office, Dad."

No, no, no! Elias made a dive for the stairs and was down in seconds. As he ran down the hallway, the second bomb went off and staggered him for a moment, but he kept running. Rico and Chase were behind him. He didn't have time to deal with Chase now. The boy was as stubborn as he was. He had to get to Maribel.

He paused at the door to the principal's office. A steel beam laid across it with cinder blocks and other debris. Electrical wires were hanging down, giving off sparks. He had to be careful. "Maribel, are you in there?"

No response, and his gut churned with a sickening feeling. Carefully, he started moving cinder blocks away.

"Oh, man." Rico said, as he came to a stop.

"Is Mom in there?" Chase asked in an unsteady voice.

Elias didn't answer. He just kept moving debris away so he could make a hole to get into the room. "Maribel! Maribel! Maribel!" he kept calling.

"Elias!"

He sagged with relief. "Are you okay?"

"Yes. But the principal needs medical attention and so do Amber and Kelly."

"We're coming."

"I love you, Elias."

He paused. *Now* she said it. And it couldn't have come at a better time. It gave him strength. He had to get her out of there.

"I love you, too. Just hold on." He clawed at the cinder blocks and Rico helped until they had a hole big enough to get in. Maribel rushed into his arms and he held her tightly for a split second. He realized she was bleeding and touched her head.

"I'm okay. It's just a scratch."

They'd debate that later. He checked on the principal and he was still alive. And then he went to the two little girls under the beam. This was going to be difficult. If he tried to move it, more debris might come down on them. "Rico, help me ease this thing up just a little so Chase and Maribel can pull them out. Just want to get it up enough to ease the pressure on their legs."

"Got it," Rico said as he grabbed hold of the beam.

"On the count of three try to lift up about an inch. Maribel and Chase, be ready to pull them out."

"Okay," they chorused.

"One. Two. Three." Elias and Rico lifted with all their strength and were only able to move it about an inch anyway, but it was enough for Chase and Maribel to pull the

girls out. He lifted the girl closest to him and placed her in Chase's arm. "You carry this one."

"It hurts," the little girl whimpered. "I want my mama."

"We're on our way. Just hold on." He looked at Rico. "Do you want to carry the principal or the other little girl?"

"I'll get the principal," Rico replied.

Elias lifted the little girl into his arms. "Let's go. Maribel, go first. Go!"

They slipped through the opening into the hallway just as another bomb went off. It shook the building and the little girls started to cry.

"Let's go! Let's go!" Elias ordered and took off down the hallway with everyone following him. When he reached the janitors closet, he said, "Rico, go first. The principal needs medical attention. Chase, you go next and then Maribel." No one questioned him and soon they were on the roof and the firemen were helping everyone down. Ambulances were waiting. Elias handed off the little girl and swung one leg over to go down the ladder. He didn't look back. He was just glad to leave this hell hole with his family alive. When he reached the bottom, he started to run because he knew the fourth bomb was about to go off. He heard the blast first. Then debris hit his back and the flying ladder brought him to the ground.

"Elias!" Maribel screamed.

He clawed his way through the rubble and two strong arms dragged him to safety. Rico and Chase helped him to his feet. Maribel wrapped her arms around him and they stood and watched as the fifth bomb went off, then the sixth and then all of them seemed to go off at once in the biggest blast Elias had ever seen. The people of Horseshoe stood in stunned silence as they watched their school go up in a plume of dark smoke.

"Let's go home," Elias said to Maribel. But they didn't

get far. The Rebel family mobbed them with hugs. Then Wyatt was there with an ambulance within six feet of him.

"I'm not going to the ER, Wyatt."

"If you don't care about yourself, you might think about Maribel. She was unconscious in there for a while. She needs to see a doctor and I'm here to see that she does. You saved my family and now I'm going to help yours."

"Wyatt…"

"Elias, I don't feel very good," Maribel murmured and Elias caught her before she slipped to the ground. In seconds, they were in the ambulance, blaring down the highway to the ER.

Elias was fine with just bruises, but Maribel had a concussion and had to undergo some tests. The waiting room filled up with news reporters wanting a story. Two hours later, Maribel was okayed to go home. She needed to rest for the next few days. Elias told the doctor he would make sure she had all the rest she needed. They slipped out a side door where Chase and Grandpa were waiting.

When they turned down Mulberry Lane, they could see all the cars and people standing in their yard. Chase zoomed into the garage and put the door down quickly. Inside, the Rebel family waited once again and they were hugged and kissed.

Elias put up his hands. "Okay. Everybody, we're okay. Maribel has a concussion and she has to rest, so would you do me a favor? I want everyone to go home and let us rest. No thanks required. Anyone would've done what I did today."

His mother shook her head. "No, son. No one would have gone into that building but you."

"Go home, everybody. And, Falcon, you're the head of the family, get those people off our lawn. Tell them I'm

all out of words and I'm not seeing anyone." He looked around. "Where's Rico? He can answer questions."

"No, way, man," Rico said. "I was just there to help you. I didn't know about the stairwell and how to get those people out. It's all you, man." Then Rico did something unexpected. He hugged Elias and Elias hugged him back in a bear hug. He was as close to Rico as he was to his brothers and he knew Rico always had his back.

It was an emotional moment. Elias grabbed Maribel's hand and they walked into the bedroom and locked the door. They took a shower together because he was afraid she would pass out again. He washed her hair and his, too. They were both filthy.

"I can wash my own hair," Maribel protested.

"You're half-asleep and you have to stay awake."

She leaned into him and her naked body against his was doing marvelous things to his own body. He reached for a towel and wrapped it around her and then towel dried her hair. Then he slipped a T-shirt over her head and tucked her into bed. He crawled in beside her and just held her, glad they were both alive.

He kissed her forehead. "Say what you said to me in the school."

She reached up and touched his face and he looked into her beautiful blue eyes. "I love you, Elias Rebel."

Gone was the sadness from her eyes. Something had happened in that room and she sat up telling him all about it. "My mother was there. I could feel her. This big weight has been lifted from my shoulders. I carried that resentment around for so long and I'm free now. Free to love you like you deserve." Her eyes sparkled.

He pushed her damp hair from her face. "I love you more than I've loved anyone in my whole life, and when Chase told me you were in the principal's office I couldn't

breathe or move for a moment as I realized I could have lost you."

"You didn't. I'm going to love you forever."

"Deal." He kissed her gently and she wrapped her arms around him, kissing him deeply in return. The kiss went on until he drew back. "I can't believe I'm saying this, but the doctor said no strenuous activity."

She curled into his body. "Then just hold me until this nightmare fades away."

"I'll hold you until the cows come home."

She raised up and looked at him, smiling. "Exactly when is that?"

He smiled back. "They never come home. You have to go get them."

"Ah."

There was a tap at the door. "Dad," Chase whispered.

"Come in, son."

"I just wanted to check on Mom."

"I'm fine," Maribel said.

"Is everybody gone?" Elias asked.

"Yes. Uncle Falcon got rid of everybody on the lawn and Uncle Quincy made everybody go home, even Grandpa."

"Grandpa went home?" That surprised Elias. He didn't think anyone could make Grandpa go home, but the old man was tired and exhausted and needed to rest, too.

"Yeah. He and Grandma are bringing breakfast in the morning." Grandpa and his mother were getting along better these days. That was a good sign.

"Dad…"

"Hmm?"

"Can I… Can I stay in here with y'all for a while? Every time I close my eyes I hear those bombs going off."

After the harrowing day everyone had been through,

Chase just wanted to be with his parents. Elias patted the bed. "Jump in."

Elias wrapped his arms around Maribel and Chase. Sleep would evade him tonight, but that didn't matter. He would rather be with the two people he loved more than anything in the world. He had everything he ever wanted. He was blessed.

Epilogue

Two weeks later

It was Christmas Day and the town of Horseshoe was celebrating the holiday on the school grounds to give thanks. The kids had put up a Christmas tree. Usually it was at the courthouse, but the decision had been made for this year to put it at the site of the school.

The bombing had been national news and donations were coming in from around the world. Services had been donated and so many other things like computers, books and desks. A crew had come in and removed all the charred remains and now there was just a dark spot on the ground where the school had once been.

Everything was coming together quickly. An architect had donated his services to draw up new plans. It would be just like the old school, except much larger and updated. A concrete company had donated concrete and a roofing company had donated the roof. Plumbing and electrical services had been donated. On the first working day in January, forms would go up and the new school would be worked on around the clock. Everyone was hoping to be in by the first of April.

That left the problem of where the kids were going to

go to school in the meantime. A contractor had a warehouse between Horseshoe and Temple and he offered the site to the school. Elias spent most of the week putting up walls to make temporary classrooms. Come January, the kids would have a place to go to school. They would have to be bussed to the warehouse, but no one complained.

Tables laden with food were scattered under the big oak trees around the school. There was camaraderie between the people. They were laughing, talking and making plans. The kids played and Chase and the other boys were throwing a ball. It was like one big family.

Elias tensed as he saw the McCray family walking toward the Rebel table. Gunnar and Malachi carried their daughters. Both girls had a leg in a cast. They were blue-eyed and blond and Elias couldn't tell them apart.

Elias got to his feet, as did Maribel. One of the girls held something out to him. It was a homemade plaque that had the girl's handprints on it. Under each handprint the name Amber and Kelly was written and the date of the school bombing. At the top was written *Thank you, Elias Rebel*.

Elias didn't know what to say.

"That's so sweet," Maribel said, kissing both the girls and hugging Cindy and Cheryl.

"Mama helped us make it," the girl Malachi was holding said. "We wanted you to know how much we appreciated you coming in and getting us."

Elias cleared his throat. "You're very welcome. I'm glad to see you are both okay."

Ira stepped forward and held out his hand. Elias didn't hesitate in shaking it. "Thank you for saving my grandchildren."

Elias nodded. He didn't feel words were needed.

Ira held a Walmart bag in his hand. He reached inside

and pulled out a small jewelry box and handed it to Maribel. "This is the brooch your mother wore that you loved. It belonged to her mother. I thought you might want it."

Take it, Maribel. Take it! End all the animosity today.

As if reading his mind, she reached out and took the box. Opening it, she said, "I always loved this brooch. Thank you."

Ira pulled a small jewelry box out with a ballerina on top of it and handed it to Rosie, who was standing next to Maribel. "You used to play with this for hours, watching the ballerina go round and round. I thought you might like to have it for your little girl."

Rosie took the box, hugged her father and said, "Thank you." Then she pointed to Phoenix, who was holding Gracie, and Jake was standing beside him. "That's our daughter, Gracie, and our son, Jake."

"You have a nice family," Ira said. The man seemed nervous, clearly not knowing what to say or do next. But it was a small step toward peace.

He turned to Elias's mother and every Rebel son was on his feet, including Jericho. "There's been a lot of bad blood between the Rebels and the McCrays."

Their mother stood with Grandpa by her side. "Yes, there has."

"I've been told most of it was on the McCray side."

"I agree."

The townspeople seemed to edge closer, eager to hear what was being said between the two feuding families of the town. Wyatt was on his feet, a few yards behind them.

"I thought I would never live to see the day a Rebel would risk his life to save a McCray."

"My son is like that. All my boys are."

Ira nodded. Again, he seemed at a loss for words.

"I have welcomed your daughters and your niece into my family and I love them as if they were my own daughters. I will spend the rest of my life loving them and my grandchildren. What will you be doing, Ira?"

He cleared his throat. "I hope someday they will let me be a small part of their lives."

"I'm sure they would like that."

"The feud doesn't seem to affect the younger generation, but for you and me, Kate, the feud will never end."

"That's true, Ira, but I don't intend to let it control my life anymore. It's time for peace, or at least an attempt at peace."

Ira nodded. "I agree." He walked away, still holding the plastic bag in his hand, and Elias would always remember this day as when the walls of anger between the Rebels and the McCrays began to crumble away. With the intermarriage of the McCrays into the Rebel family, they would now be one big family. Things wouldn't be easy, but at least they were now willing to get along and share the future.

He pulled Maribel to his side. "Miracles do happen."

"Yeah." She looked to where the school had once stood. "Sometimes you have to lose everything to realize what you have."

His arm tightened around her. "I love you."

She smiled up at him. "I love you, too. And I will show you just how much later."

"I'm counting on it." He kissed her lips.

The town of Horseshoe had survived a tragedy and it would go on, just like the Rebels and the McCrays would go on. But it would be different. It would be better. The future beamed like a bright star. All they had to do was reach up and grab it. Life was good in Horseshoe, Texas.

Elias gave thanks as the town gathered around the Christmas tree to sing "Silent Night." It was a Christmas no one would ever forget.

* * * * *

#1673 THE BULL RIDER'S VALENTINE

Mustang Valley • by Cathy McDavid

When Nate Truett and Ronnie Hartman are thrown together to help with the local rodeo, they are still healing from a tragic past. Yet an old attraction prevails. Will a Valentine's Day proposal bring them together for good?

#1674 COWBOY LULLABY

The Boones of Texas • by Sasha Summers

Years ago, cowboy Click Hale broke Tandy Boone's heart. Now he's her neighbor and a father to a beautiful daughter. How can Tandy start over with a reminder of everything she lost living right next door?

#1675 WRANGLING CUPID'S COWBOY

Saddle Ridge, Montana • by Amanda Renee

Rancher and single dad Garrett Slade can't stop thinking about Delta Grace, the beautiful farrier who works for him. He's finally ready to take the next step, but he senses she has a secret...

#1676 THE BULL RIDER'S TWIN TROUBLE

Spring Valley, Texas • by Ali Olson

Bull rider Brock McNeal loves to live on the edge. But when he starts to fall for Cassie Stanford, a widow with twin boys, Brock's in a whole different kind of danger!

Dear Reader,

This is the seventh and last book in the Texas Rebels series. The stories are based on how the Rebel brothers deal with life and love after the death of their father.

Elias is the lone bachelor. Work, women and beer define Elias. He's known to be tough as rawhide and says he'll never get married and be tied down like his brothers. He enjoys his freedom. That is, until Maribel McCray returns to Horseshoe, Texas.

Maribel's down on her luck and striving to put her life back together. She and Elias were attracted to each other in high school, but because of their feuding families they stayed away from each other. When Maribel's son gets arrested, she asks Elias for help. He tells her she would have to give him a good reason for him to help her. She gives him one he's not expecting and it turns his world upside down.

This is a story about second chances and things that could've been. A lot happens in this book and I hope it keeps you captivated to the big ending. It's time to say goodbye to the Rebel family and the characters I've lived with for three years. It's kind of sad, but my mind is moving forward to more characters and more books.

Until then, with love and thanks,

Linda

PS: You can email me at Lw1508@aol.com; send me a message on Facebook.com/lindawarrenauthor or on Twitter, @texauthor; write me at PO Box 5182, Bryan, TX 77805; or visit my website at lindawarren.net. Your mail and thoughts are deeply appreciated.

Cast of Characters

Kate Rebel: Matriarch of the Rebel family.

Falcon: The eldest son—the strong one. Reunited with his wife, Leah, and proud father of Eden and John.

Egan: The loner. Married to Rachel Hollister, daughter of the man who put him in jail. Son Justin.

Quincy: The peacemaker. Married to Jenny Walker, his childhood best friend. Daughter Martha Kate.

Elias: The fighter. Falls in love with the daughter of his family's archenemy.

Paxton: The lover. Found his forever love with Remi Roberts and their adopted daughter, Annie.

Jude: The serious, responsible one. Back together with his first love, Paige Wheeler, and raising their son, Zane.

Phoenix: The youngest Rebel challenges his own family when he falls in love with the enemy—Rosemary McCray. Father of Jake.

Abraham (Abe) Rebel: Paternal grandfather.

Jericho Johnson: Egan's friend from prison.